For fifteen minutes, not a shot had been fired. The police maneuvered on the street, trying to get all the civilians out of the line of fire and to evacuate the buildings so no one would get hurt by stray bullets if the gunman decided to start shooting out windows.

They were stopped four blocks away by a police officer wearing an orange vest and standing in the middle of the street.

Tynan nodded and said, "Sorry. I'm Lieutenant Mark Tynan of the United States Navy, and I think the man you have trapped up there is one of mine."

"You have any idea what he's doing up there?"

"I haven't the foggiest notion," Tynan lied. "But if it is one of my men, you won't get to him until he's ready for you to get to him . . ."

SNIPER

SEALS
#10
SNIPER

STEVE MACKENZIE

AVON BOOKS ▲ NEW YORK

SEALS #10: SNIPER is an original publication of Avon Books. This work has never before appeared in book form. This work is a novel. Any similarity to actual persons or events is purely concidental.

AVON BOOKS
A division of
The Hearst Corporation
105 Madison Avenue
New York, New York 10016

Copyright © 1988 by Kevin D. Randle
Published by arrangement with the author
Library of Congress Catalog Card Number: 88-91577
ISBN: 0-380-75533-5

First Avon Books Printing: November 1988

AVON TRADEMARK REG. U.S. PAT. OFF. AND IN OTHER COUNTRIES, MARCA REGISTRADA, HECHO EN U.S.A.

Printed in the U.S.A.

K–R   10   9   8   7   6   5   4   3   2   1

1

The wind was blowing out. That was evident by the score which had the Cubs up by seven runs and still batting in the third inning. Navy Lieutenant Mark Tynan sat in a fairly uncomfortable chair with a stiff back and cigarette burns on it, his feet propped on the bed, and watched as another fly ball sailed over the ivy-covered wall and the chain-link fence behind the bleachers to land on the street. Three more runs crossed the plate as the camera cut to the kids who were chasing down the souvenir.

Tynan, a young man who was just over six feet tall, had a deep tan from the recent time spent in the tropics. Tynan had blue eyes and dark hair that was longer than regulations said it should be. He was a slender man who was sitting there in khaki pants, blue shirt and dark shoes. Not the Ho Chi Minh sandals made of truck tires that were the rage on college campuses, but leather things that looked nothing like those made in Vietnam.

He was wondering what to do with the rest of the afternoon and wondered why he hadn't gone down to Wrigley Field to watch the game in person. Television was fine and the instant replays made it possible to see things that he missed as he glanced through the paper or stared out the window, but there just wasn't a hell of a lot to do

1

in a motel room. Sometimes it seemed more confining than a prison cell, even with its color TV, telephone and vibrating bed.

Tynan stood and moved to the window that looked out over a parking lot that was mostly vacant in the middle of the afternoon. Sunlight flashed from a couple of windshields. A young couple, dressed in shorts and T-shirts, walked along the sidewalk hand in hand, ignoring the traffic on the street near them and the roar of jets on the approach path to O'Hare.

There was a sudden cheer from the TV and Tynan turned in time to see another fly ball make it to the street. The Cubs now had a twelve run lead and the flags were standing straight out. The score was beginning to look like something from a football game: twenty-one to seven.

"Christ," said Tynan. "I've got to get out of here. If only for an hour."

But there wasn't any place to go or anything for him to do. Class did not start until the following Monday, and home and family were too far away for a quick visit. The only alternative was to wander the halls of the motel, and that was even more depressing than staying in the room. He returned to the chair and sat down, focusing on the television.

The knock at the door came as a welcome surprise. He was going to shout at it, telling whoever was out there to come on in, but instead walked over to open it. Doors in motels were set to lock automatically.

Ignoring the peephole, Tynan turned the knob and stepped back as he opened the door. The person standing there was not who he had expected.

"What the hell are you doing here?"

"Thank you, Mark. I'm very happy to see you too. I drop everything I'm doing so that I can fly up for a visit, bribe fourteen different people, and that's the best reception I can get?"

Tynan closed the door and watched as Stevie King walked into the room, glanced at the bed and then sat down in the only chair. She put her purse on the small desk, crossed her legs slowly and said, "Well?"

Tynan studied her closely. A tall, slim woman with long, light brown hair, now bleached nearly blonde by the same tropical sun he'd been under. She had blue eyes and thin features, her nose almost pointed. She smiled, showing perfect teeth. She wore a white blouse and a short, dark blue skirt and hadn't bothered with stockings.

Tynan moved toward the TV and turned down the sound. The Cubs had finished batting, but the run production in the game didn't seem to let up. The opposite side had two runners on and the batter had just put a foul ball into the stands four hundred feet away.

"Well," said Tynan, "I'm glad to see you, Stevie."

"Glad to see me," she said shaking her head. "You overwhelm me."

Tynan couldn't help smiling. "Let me get over the surprise, first. I'm more than a little surprised. Now, I'm damn glad to see you. Just how in the hell did you find me?"

"Not that hard. I called your parents and they said you were in Chicago still, just as you said you'd be, and I did a little detective work from there. And then flew on up."

Tynan sat on the bed and studied her carefully. She was a good-looking woman who seemed to have just escaped for summer break from college. Tynan knew that it wasn't true and that she held a Ph.D. in cultural anthropology. She taught on the faculty of the college.

"You know," he said, "that I'm assigned to a school here that begins in the morning."

"School?" she repeated. "What kind of school?"

Tynan scratched at the back of his neck and glanced at the TV screen where the players were parading around the diamond again, suggesting that another ball had escaped from the park. "That's a damned fine question, because I don't have the faintest notion."

"Oh, so it's classified," said King, winking at him in a conspiratorial manner.

"No, it's not that. If it had been classified, I could have told you that. I just don't know what in the hell it's about."

King recrossed her legs, letting the hem of her skirt ride higher on her thigh. She grinned evilly then and sat back in the chair. "So what had you planned on doing before class began in the morning?"

"Not a hell of a lot." He leaned forward and turned off the TV, even as another ball bounced on the street to the delight of the kids waiting there to grab it.

King got to her feet and stepped closer to Tynan. She felt his lips brush hers and said, "Finally, a hello kiss."

"Caught me off guard."

"Thought all you SEALS were supposed to be fast on your feet, quicker than lightning and more deadly than a cobra."

He slipped a hand between them, found one of the buttons on her blouse and undid it. He let his fingers push the material out of the way and felt the soft, smoothness of her skin.

"Aren't you getting a little ahead of yourself here?" she asked breathlessly.

"I can always stop," said Tynan.

"Oh, no. I didn't mean to imply that you should stop."

Tynan attacked the rest of the buttons and slipped the blouse from her shoulders. She smiled and stepped closer so that Tynan could reach around her. He glanced over his shoulder so that he could see the hooks on her bra. When he had it unfastened, she let it slide down her arms and drop to the floor. She then unhooked her skirt and let it fall away, pooling around her feet.

She took a step to the rear and sat on the bed. She leaned back on her elbows and looked up. "Well?"

Tynan stood there and looked at her nearly naked body. It was a good body, with no fat on it. A slender body, lightly tanned, a pale band around her hips, but not one on her chest. She sunbathed without a top. He didn't want to move or to talk. He just wanted to stand there and look at her.

"Well?" she said again.

Tynan unbuttoned his shirt and took it off. He sat down next to her and kicked off his shoes and then pulled off his socks. He rolled to his side, pulled her toward him and then kissed her deeply.

"Now," she said, quietly. "Now."

An hour later, Tynan was worn out. He looked up at the ceiling and felt his heart hammering in his chest. There was a coating of sweat on his body that was soaking into the bedspread. He glanced to the left. King lay on her side, an arm under her cheek, her hair damp with sweat.

"Wow," she said. "That was quite . . . a workout."

"Oh, yeah," said Tynan. "Oh, yeah. Quite the workout."

She rolled to her back and put her hands under her head. She took a deep breath and let it out slowly. "Now, what is the plan of the day?"

Tynan finally forced himself to sit up and then looked at her naked body. He tore his eyes away and said, "I think that we should get something to eat and then I've got to get some rest. Class starts tomorrow."

"Uh-huh."

"What are you planning to do? You have a room?"

"Well," she said, waving a hand, "I think I have one."

Tynan couldn't help smiling. "Okay, but did you plan to get one of your own?"

"Do I need one of my own?"

Tynan stood and snagged his pants off the floor. He was going to put them on but decided that he needed a shower first. He draped the pants over the back of the chair. "You're certainly welcome to stay here, if you want."

"Your enthusiasm is simply overwhelming." She pushed her damp hair from her forehead. There were beads of sweat at her hairline, on her upper lip and across her chest.

"Dinner," said Tynan, trying to divert the conversation and his attention from her body.

"We should have some."

"Great," said Tynan. He disappeared into the bathroom and turned on the shower, holding a hand under the spray to test the temperature. He played with the faucets until he had it where he wanted it and then pulled the curtain closed, but he stayed on the outside. He turned and looked at himself in the mirror.

King appeared in the doorway and said, "You never told me what this class is all about."

"You going to join me in the shower?"

"Of course, but you're not going to dodge the question that easily."

Tynan unwrapped the soap and tossed the paper into the tiny wastebasket tucked under the counter. "But I told you as much as I know. Some kind of special training that the Navy ordered me to attend. They gave us no indication about it. I can speculate but I don't have any real idea."

King passed him, pulled the curtain aside and stepped into the tub, moving forward so that she was under the spray. She ducked her head, letting the water soak her hair as she fanned it out.

Tynan joined her, stepping close, his hands on her shoulders. He took the washcloth she handed him and washed her back carefully, slowly. When she turned, he did the same things to her chest and belly. They took turns washing one another and when they finished, they took turns drying each other just as slowly.

Then they went out for dinner. They ate slowly and sat at the table, drinking wine and talking. Not much time had passed since they had last been together, but they still had a lot to catch up on. Tynan was interested in what had been learned about the Mayan city they had discovered in Honduras. A lost city, still inhabited by descendants of the Mayans but virtually unknown to the outside, modern world.

Stevie King, holding a wine glass in one hand, leaned back, glanced at the ceiling and then told Tynan exactly what they had learned about the Mayans. Things that had been suspected were now confirmed. The reason for the mass exodus from some of the cities was now known, and there were indications that the Mayans had told their descendants about their hidden treasures. King thought that another expedition into Honduras might uncover them.

She leaned forward, put the glass down and said, "You'd be surprised about it. There is such a richness of information. We're learning so much." She lowered her voice. "And I'm really not supposed to talk about it. If the fortune hunters learned about this, they'd swarm over the area like vultures. The loss to science would be impossible to calculate."

"That's fine," said Tynan. He wanted to know more about it, but not right at that moment. There were other things intruding. "You want to get out of here?"

"Sure."

They returned to the motel and as Tynan locked the

door, King turned on the television. She sat down and stared at it, watching the news.

"Anything interesting going on?"

She shook her head as the pictures of helicopters landing in a rice paddy came on. The reporter was talking about a major sweep and rising American casualties in the war in Southeast Asia.

"When's it going to end?" she asked.

"I don't know," said Tynan. "When it's politically expedient for the administration to end it. When the President will reap the largest reward for getting us out."

"You don't really believe that, do you?"

Tynan dropped into the chair and took off his shoes. He glanced at the screen, but the newscaster had already moved on to another story. He shrugged then and said, "I'm afraid that I do believe it."

"Then why do you stay in the Navy?"

The last thing that Tynan wanted to do was get into a discussion of politics and the war with a woman who taught at a university. Their opinions and thoughts had to be a hundred and eighty degrees out of phase. There was no common ground. She believed the war in Vietnam was wrong, and Tynan was one of those who had to fight it.

"I stay in the Navy because it's my job."

She smiled at that and said, "But it can't be that challenging for a man of your intelligence."

Tynan felt his blood boil because she was asking the question that his parents had asked when he had visited them. It was the question that his friends in the business world asked when they put down their drinks long enough to talk. They all said that because he was intelligent, he should get out of the Navy and find a real job. Build a career selling shoes or radios or cars and worry about production quotas and sales figures and keeping the grass green around his house.

Then he laughed and said, "If you want to talk about this, we can, but I'd rather just go to bed."

"Someday we're going to have to deal with this. I think that you're wasting your talents in the Navy."

"Okay," snapped Tynan, a little more harshly than he meant to. "The Navy may not be the best career in the world, but it is mine. So far it has been interesting and as challenging as anything that you could name. I don't know from one day to the next what is going to happen." He grinned again and added, "Besides all that, if it hadn't been for the Navy, we never would have met. You have to admit that my talents were of great value in Honduras."

"Mark," she said quietly, "I don't want to fight about this. It's just that I have a problem with what you do and what you represent."

"Just remember one thing," said Tynan, leaning forward, his elbows on his knees, "I don't represent anything. My opinions and beliefs have nothing to do with the job I do. I'm like the TV station forced to carry political messages that don't necessarily reflect the views and opinions of that station."

"But how, in good conscience, can you do that?" she asked.

Tynan ran a hand through his hair and stared at the floor. "Because I'm willing to serve in the Navy means that you can sit there and make those statements. We buy that freedom with our service." He held up a hand to stop her protest. "Sometimes we're called on to do things that may not be right, or may not be moral, to the way some people think, but because we're there, willing to do that, they can make their pronouncements. I think serving in the Navy is one of the best things that I can do. It offers me an opportunity to do something that I enjoy. It offers me a chance to get paid for something I enjoy."

He looked up and studied her again. The light blouse

molded itself to the curve of her breast. He looked at her legs and then down at her thin ankles. He'd done it again: gotten into a political discussion with a beautiful woman.

"I don't understand you," she said. "I don't understand at all."

Tynan moved toward her and pulled her to her feet so that he could kiss her. "You don't have to understand. You just have to be here."

"And you don't care that I'm in the street protesting the war?"

"Oh, hell yes," said Tynan. "I care, but what I do ensures that you can hit the street protesting. I may think that you're misguided in your protests, but you have the right to do that, and it's one of the reasons that I'm in the Navy."

She threw her arms around him and kissed him, forcing her tongue into his mouth. She held on and then finally released him. "If you can take that, then I can take what you do."

"At least it's interesting," said Tynan.

He had no idea how interesting it was going to get when the school started the next morning.

2

Jason Bainbridge sat in his office, a cup of steaming coffee near his left hand, and studied the reports that had gathered overnight. He blinked in the bright light from overhead and then rocked back so that he could put his feet up on the desk top. A burnt-orange wall that formed the front of his cubicle stopped short of the ceiling. To one side, on the top of his desk was a phone, a stack of in-out baskets, an appointment calendar and several books.

Bainbridge was a young man with long hair and a neatly trimmed black beard. He had small bright eyes, an eyebrow that covered both eyes and met over the bridge of his nose and an intense look. He was a small man with wide shoulders and narrow hips. He had on a worn and faded blue work shirt and worn and faded blue jeans. His feet were slightly dirty in his Ho Chi Minh sandals.

During the six months he had worked at the firm, there had been suggestions that he clean up his act or he would be out on his ear. He had ignored them, telling the boss that what a man wore did not equate his worth as a human being or his ability to do his job. His clothes were comfortable and when he was comfortable, he worked harder. "And isn't that what it's all about?"

"That and the proper image," said the man, staring up at Bainbridge.

"But we're an advertising agency, for Christ's sake. It's not like we're actually doing something that will help the human race. We're not performing brain surgery or searching for the cure to cancer."

"If that's your attitude, maybe you'd better find yourself another job."

Bainbridge had come close to walking out then, just as he had come close to punching the man in the face. He had wanted to hammer the man into oblivion. He had wanted to see him spit broken teeth as blood washed over his face. He had wanted to see him lying on the floor as Bainbridge tried to kick his head in, but that hadn't happened. Instead, Bainbridge, realizing that he would need the job for another six months, had held his anger in check.

He had swallowed his pride, confessed that he understood and had gone home to change. But slowly he had slipped into his old habits, and if it hadn't been for the quality of his work, they would have fired him. If it hadn't been for the number of political candidates who used the agency's services, Bainbridge would have quit.

He stood up and stretched, looking over the top of the wall, and saw a sea of empty desks. No one ever got in before eight. They sometimes stayed until midnight, but they didn't come in early. Bainbridge left his cubicle and walked among the desks and cubes, checking out the material and files left in the open. He read some of them, made a few notes and then returned to his own desk.

He was amazed at the things people confessed to the ad agency. Deeds that would put them out of office if the public knew. Deeds that were dark and disgusting and the perfect thing for blackmail. A politician who needed public support couldn't stand the slightest smear to his name but still confessed all to the agency so they could be prepared for damage control, if that became necessary. It was almost as if they had a need to confess to someone, and the ad agency was the perfect place to do it. Since the agency wanted the business, they overlooked the man's shortcomings.

Bainbridge unlocked the bottom drawer of his desk and added a few facts to the already huge file of little things that could help him build his career. They ranged from the man who liked to visit prostitutes and take pictures of their crotches, to the man who had been caught shoplifting as a teenager. Not much really, but damaging in the times of campaign when the smallest indiscretion could mean a defeat.

Just as he was closing the drawer and locking it, the door to the office opened and a young woman entered. She was tall, five eight or nine, had long straight hair and blue eyes. Bainbridge didn't know her name, but he knew that she worked there, lost in the sea of humanity that kept the doors of the agency opened. She was a cold, aluff woman who rarely talked to her fellow employees.

Bainbridge stepped out of his cube, stretched, raising his hands high over his head and said, "Good morning."

"Morning," she said as she took off her light jacket and hung it up.

"You're in early," he said.

She turned and looked at him and then shrugged. She stepped around him and moved to the opposite end of the huge room, turning on a small fluorescent light that sat on her desk. She didn't look back or say anything else.

"Bitch," muttered Bainbridge. He stood there, watching her back for a moment, and wondered how it would feel to slip his fingers around her neck and begin to squeeze, slowly at first, then tighter and tighter until her face turned red and then blue as she struggled to breathe.

"Most satisfying," he said quietly and then returned to

his desk. The woman would be sorry that she had snubbed him. She and everyone else would one day wish that they had been kinder, nicer to him because he wasn't going to remain a fifth-rate worker in a third-rate agency in a second-rate city. Someday things would change for him. That was the purpose of the files and the information and his hanging on in the dead-end job that he hated so passionately.

"Not for money," he said to himself.

Never for money, because money was too easy to spend and was too quickly gone. Money could buy friends, but when the cash had vanished, so did the friends. No, he just wanted to be friends with some of the men and women whose names graced his private files. A kind word from them, in the right place at the right time, and he would be moving up into positions of importance and prominence.

Tynan was up with the sun. He climbed slowly, carefully out of bed and then stood at the bathroom door looking back. King lay on her side, facing him, the sheets arranged so that he could see a bare shoulder and a bare thigh. He studied her for a moment and wished that the damned school didn't start for another twenty-four hours. He could think of things that he would rather do.

Inside the bathroom, he turned on the light and then brushed his teeth. He filled the sink with hot water, shaved and then washed his face. He donned the uniform that he had hung on the back of the door the night before so that he could dress without waking King. Finished, he left that room and moved carefully to his suitcase.

"How long before you have to leave?" asked King in a voice fogged by sleep.

"Don't know. Jacobs is going to come by and pick me up. He's got an official car."

She threw off the sheet and then sat up, not bothering to cover herself. "You sure that he'll be here *soon*?"

Tynan shook his head and then studied the floor as if the patterns in the rug had become fascinating. "I'm afraid he'll be here soon. Much too soon."

King started to stretch, lifting her hands high over her head and arching her back. Then, almost as if to prove that Tynan's information had been right, there was a knock on the door.

Tynan turned and looked at it. "He's arrived."

King leaped from the bed and scurried into the bathroom. She started to close the door and then peeked around it. "See you tonight?"

"Of course." Tynan moved to the door and opened it. "Come on in," he told the big man.

Donald Jacobs was a chief petty officer in the Navy and, like Tynan, a SEAL. He had black hair, brown eyes and a round, almost moon-shaped face. He spoke with a husky voice and in a Southern accent. The tattoo on the inside of his left forearm, was the result of a fight in Saigon and then a trip to the tattoo parlor. It said *Sat Cong,* and almost no one knew what that meant.

"Ya'all about ready?" asked Jacobs.

Tynan turned to the combination TV stand and luggage rack, picked up his cap and checked the lieutenant's bars fastened to it. As he put it on, he said, "All ready."

Jacobs grinned at him and then knocked on the bathroom door. "Morning, Dr. King."

As they closed the door and entered the hallway, Tynan began to laugh. "Oh that was a dirty trick. And what if it hadn't been Stevie?"

"Well, sir, I heard her voice and recognized it. Figured I'd give her something to think about today. Keep her on her toes, so to speak."

"Thanks a lot," said Tynan.

They left the motel and stepped into the bright light of the early morning. There was a chill in the air and a light fog that was burning off quickly. Jacobs took him to the light gray car that said *U. S. Navy* on the door. Just under it was the warning, *For official use only*.

Jacobs unlocked the passenger's door and Tynan climbed in, leaning across to open the driver's side. As Jacobs climbed behind the wheel, he asked, "You have any idea what this whole thing is about?"

Tynan shrugged and said, "I haven't heard a thing. I was hoping that you knew something. I thought all you CPOs stuck together sharing information."

Jacobs started the engine, dropped the car into gear and pulled forward, toward the parking lot exit. As he watched the traffic, waiting for a spot to open, he said, "This is the first time that I haven't gotten something early from one of my friends. Hell, everyone talks about the schools, but no one knows shit about this one."

Tynan looked at his watch and said, "We'll know more in about an hour."

They had been taken to a small classroom at the Glenview Naval Air Station. It was an old building with dirty tile on the floor, walls painted in a faded gray and light fixtures that hung from a ceiling ten feet over their heads. The classroom had three rows of tables, chairs on one side facing the front where there was a raised platform and a lectern. Behind the lectern was a blackboard, but nothing was written on it.

Tynan and Jacobs had been the first to arrive and had been escorted to the room by a yeoman who looked as if he still belonged in high school. He opened the door to the classroom and told them, "Take any seat. The instructor will be here in just a few minutes."

As the yeoman left, Tynan searched the room, but there

was absolutely nothing in it to give him a clue about the nature of the class. The posters on the walls were standard Navy-issue. How to wear the uniform and the ribbons and one that suggested Naval Aviation was a career for the future. And a large painting of Naval Aviation destroying the Japanese fleet at Midway during the Second World War.

Tynan moved to the front and took a seat close to the bank of windows that looked out on a parking lot. ''Well, we still don't know shit.''

Jacobs took the chair next to Tynan and turned as the door opened. Two more men entered, both enlisted. One of them was a huge, beefy man who looked as if he played professional football. The other was smaller and darker.

''What in hell is going on here?'' asked the big man.

''We were hoping that you'd be able to tell us,'' said Tynan. He stood and held out a hand. ''Tynan.''

''Dennis Davis,'' said the big man.

''Bruce Harison,'' said the other.

''This is Donald Jacobs,'' said Tynan. ''Where are you all coming from?''

''Coronado,'' said Davis.

Two more men entered then. They were a Mutt and Jeff pair, one of them tall and thin and the other shorter and stockier. The tall one had black hair and dark eyes, and the shorter had brown hair and brown eyes. Both looked as young as the yeoman who brought them in so that it was beginning to look like a high school reunion. The taller was named Alan Meyer and the shorter was Charles Starkey.

They took seats and sat quietly for a few moments. Meyer suspected that they were being groomed for some kind of covert mission into North Vietnam, but Tynan shot that down.

''We wouldn't be here if we were. We'd be in Washington or in California. At the least, the facilities would be a little more secure than this.''

Meyer nodded and fell silent.

Finally the door opened for the last time. A small man in a gray suit entered. He carried a zippered portfolio and walked straight to the front of the room. He had black hair that looked as if it had been oiled and a full beard. He wore black horn-rimmed glasses. He didn't speak as he moved to the front. With precise, measured movements, he set his case on the lectern and opened it with three short strokes. The zipper rasped as the men waited.

When he finished, he looked up and then said, ''Is this everyone?''

Tynan looked at the others and then shrugged. ''We don't have a clue.''

''Yes.'' The man pulled a sheet of paper from his case, looked at Tynan and said, ''You're the lieutenant?''

''Tynan, yes.''

He called the roll and then put the list away. He turned, saw that there was no chalk for the blackboard and shrugged. He leaned on the lectern, his hands clasped, and stared at the dirty floor.

''My name, for those of you who don't know, is Harlan Sumner-Gleason and it is my task to train your minds in a few of the new techniques that have been learned in the last couple of years. The course syllabus calls for three weeks of instruction and practical experience before you're returned to your respective units, unless things progress at a high level. Then your assistance can be extended for a longer period.''

Tynan nodded as Sumner-Gleason spoke, but the words were nearly meaningless. They said nothing other than that Tynan and the men were stuck in the classroom in Chicago for a minimum of three weeks.

Sumner-Gleason spoke for a few minutes more, saying

the same basic thing but never telling them what they would be studying. He spoke about a special diet that would be distributed and used for the first week. Later, another would be given to them to guide their eating for that point on, and he expected them to follow it for the rest of their naval careers. He talked of special exercises and special training and mind-altering techniques that did not require the use of drugs. Everything would be natural.

When he wound down, he stood up straight and began shifting the papers around in front of him. With everything arranged, he launched into the class immediately. His voice boomed dramatically as he lowered it an octave for emphasis.

"First," he said, "you can get rid of the coffee and cigarettes. During the period of this instruction, I will tolerate no coffee, no alcohol and no smoking."

"Now wait a minute," said Davis, getting to his feet. "You can't come waltzing in here and suddenly tell us that we have to break the habits of a lifetime. Just who in hell are you anyway?"

Sumner-Gleason grinned as if he had expected the resistance. "I have, in my case here, orders that come from your various commanding officers and from your Bureau of Personnel. It dictates that you will accept my instructions completely and follow them to the letter. You will not sneak off and drink coffee and smoke cigarettes because I will be able to tell if you have, and you can be court-martialed for it for the breach of training."

"Oh, bullshit," said Davis.

"No bullshit," said Sumner-Gleason. "I have the appropriate documents, and the highest priority has been assigned to this project. Men of your background and training are not wasted in worthless and futile gestures. No, gentlemen, this is no bullshit."

He stared at Davis until the big man sat down again and

then said, "Let me phrase this in the vernacular. You fuck around with me and I'll have your ass in my briefcase."

Before things could get too far out of hand, Tynan stood up. He glanced at the other men, waiting for them to turn their attention to him, and then said, "You haven't told us much about this assignment. What exactly are we going to be doing for three weeks?"

"During the next three weeks," said Sumner-Gleason trying to sound important, "we are going to be training your minds and we are going to be working on developing and enhancing your esper capacity."

"Our what?" demanded Harison.

"Your ability to use extrasensory perception in your normal military duties."

"Oh, bullshit," said Davis again.

3

Bainbridge sat there for ten or fifteen minutes and felt the rage burn through him. He stared at the burnt orange of the divider and tried to bore a hole through it with his eyes. The woman had no right to snub him. It wasn't like she was someone important or even very special. She was just another lowly worker, a drone who came and went with the rest of them. Her sweat was no sweeter than anyone else's.

He stood up and looked over the top of the wall. She was still sitting there, trying to look so important and busy. Trying to impress the boss with her loyalty and her dedication. Bainbridge moved around the wall and through the maze of aisles, his eyes focused on the nape of her neck. As he approached, he could see the fine brown hairs that were swept upward into the complex, interwoven hairdo.

She didn't hear him coming. Her attention was focused on the papers in front of her. One hand gripped a cup filled with coffee and the other held a yellow pencil that she tapped against her forehead.

Bainbridge stepped right up behind her and looked over her shoulder, reading the paper that she studied. Some bullshit about the demographics for the audience of a local show. They weren't capturing the all-important teenage market who had more disposable income than the lower-status adults who would be watching. Targeting should be changed in that specific time slot for the show.

As she lifted the cup to her lips, Bainbridge grabbed her by the neck. He lifted, the muscles of his arm bunching with the effort. She came up easily with a grunt of pain and surprise. The cup tumbled from her fingers, splashing on the desk and her file folders.

"Hey!" she gasped.

Bainbridge spun her and caught her, forcing his lips to hers. She put a hand against his chest and pushed, but he just pulled at her harder, holding her tighter, almost squeezing the breath from her.

She struggled, pulling and then pushing, but she was caught tightly in his bear hug, her head tilted back as she tried to avoid his lips. She jerked right and left, but it did no good. Then she brought one knee up abruptly, as if by accident.

Bainbridge felt a flash of pain of the almost effective blow. He pushed her away from him and bent at the waist, supporting himself on the corner of her desk. His face was a pasty white and there was the sudden sweat of pain on his forehead. He raised his head slowly, his eyes ablaze with liquid fire.

"There was no reason for that," he hissed.

"Stay away from me or I'm going to the boss."

Bainbridge raised his voice to a high, squeaky pitch. "I'm going to tell." Then a blackness descended over him. He was looking at her through the wrong end of a telescope. She was a shadowy, threatening figure in the distance. Without thinking, he balled a fist and swung. There was pain in his fingers and hand and a satisfying pop.

The woman staggered back, a hip against her desk.

There was a wetness spreading on her face as the pain blossomed and expanded. Her eyes were hot with tears.

"You say a word to anyone, bitch, and I'll beat you senseless. I'll pound your head into a pulp, and if you're lucky I'll kill you."

She dropped to her knees, a hand covered in blood from her nose. She looked up at him and said, "Please."

Bainbridge stared down at her. The front of her blouse was red from blood and the sleeve stained brown from the coffee she had spilled. One of the stockings had run, showing pale skin. He felt the rage and hate course through him and wanted to reach down to pound on her. He wanted to see her lying on the floor unable to move, bleeding from a dozen wounds.

But then calm reason took over. If he did, he would be out of a job and he would find himself set back in his plans. He would spend a year or two trying to repair the damage that was so unnecessary. It had been a momentary lapse, one that could be covered if he could impress on her the importance of keeping her mouth shut.

Her head was bowed now and she had one hand to her face, trying to stop the flow of blood. For a moment Bainbridge hesitated, unsure of the next move. He wanted to reinforce what he had told her, but he didn't want to push too hard, afraid that she would panic and talk. That she would go to tell the boss as she had threatened. He turned and left her sitting on the floor, crying.

A few minutes later she stumbled by him, heading for the door. She didn't glance his way and he pretended not to notice her. The next few hours would tell. If the police arrived, or if he was summoned into the boss's office, he would know that she had talked. If not, it meant that she had been sufficiently scared by him and that everything would work out just fine. As long as she didn't talk.

As soon as the outer door closed, he rocked back in his

chair and laced his fingers behind his head. He laughed out loud and felt great. If anyone had asked him why, he wouldn't have been able to define it exactly. He would have mumbled something about bending another person to his will, forcing her to obey his orders, even when it was so obvious that something should be done to him.

That was what it was all about. Making other people do what you wanted them to do. Forcing your will on them and having them take it because you were so much more powerful and so much smarter than they were.

The day had started much better than he'd had any reason to hope it would.

The first hour of the lecture was only a history of the study of ESP, including the Rhine studies at Duke University. They looked at the suggestion that some people have an ability to read minds, predict the future, communicate over long distances, move small objects with their minds, and even a brief talk of ghosts. It was a discussion designed to open the mind to the realm of the paranormal. But in the end, it contained only anecdotal science and nothing of substance.

Tynan sat there and listened to the lecture, wondering if someone was pulling a gag. An elaborate gag. But he couldn't figure out why the Navy would spend several thousand dollars on the joke.

Sumner-Gleason kept right on talking, telling of predictions that came true and mind reading that worked, documented cases that defied explanation.

"Established science has a tendency to dismiss, out of hand, anything that it finds hard to accept. Science needs something that can be taken into the laboratory and measured. It needs something that can be duplicated time and again. And, because of the charlatans, science rejects, out of hand, claims from the paranormal."

"If that is true," asked Davis, "then how did you convince the Navy to fund this course?"

Davis leaned forward on his notes and clasped his hands together as he stared at the floor. "I'm afraid that the Navy came up with this on their own. It is designed to facilitate communication among members of the teams during the underwater activities."

Davis roared with laughter and said, "I thought that was why we had radios."

Sumner-Gleason grinned and shrugged but still looked slightly self-conscious. "I can only tell you what I know. It is their belief that an enhanced esper capacity will be of benefit to you." He glanced at his watch. "If there are no further questions, let's take a ten-minute break. Be back in your seats by seven after the hour."

As Sumner-Gleason headed out the door, Jacobs turned to Tynan and asked, "Just what in hell do they expect from this? We can't be expected to take it seriously."

Davis pushed his way to the front and sat on the table in front of Tynan. "Well, sir, what do you say?"

"Don't look at me," said Tynan. "I don't think I accept this hocus-pocus any better than the rest of you."

"But what's the purpose behind this?" asked Jacobs. "That crap about being able to communicate better underwater just doesn't hold up. We've hand signals and radios that allow us to do that."

Tynan shrugged and said, "You all know as much about it as I do."

Davis sat down close to them and said, "I think there is something to this ESP."

"So what?" snapped Jacobs. "It makes no difference that we believe in it or not. It's not something that's going to help us complete our missions."

Tynan spoke up then. "You all know as well as I do that strange things happen out there in the field. I know a guy who could follow people through the jungle without fail. If the trail vanished, he was always able to think of something, and that would get us where we wanted to go. No one could explain how he did it. Hell, he couldn't explain how he did it.''

''That doesn't make it ESP,'' said Jacobs. ''Maybe he picked up clues that were so subtle that he didn't consciously see them. A bent blade of grass or something like that. Enough of those kinds of things that he could figure it out, he just wasn't aware of the process.''

Meyer, who had been sitting there quietly, said, ''Then how do you explain this? A friend of mine, David Thompson, one day decided that he was going to get killed. He gave away everything he owned, told his friends how he wanted the funeral handled and where he wanted to be buried. Two hours later he was dead in an ambush.''

''Oh, come on,'' said Jacobs.

''I was there,'' countered Meyer.

Starkey shook his head as if trying to ward off the evil spirits and said, ''Anyone want a Coke?''

Tynan pulled a handful of change out of his pocket and said, ''Sure, I'll take one.''

''That instructor said we weren't supposed to eat or drink anything that wasn't on the official diet,'' said Harison.

''They haven't given it to us yet,'' said Tynan, ''and I want a Coke.''

Starkey picked up the money and left the classroom. As he did, Meyer asked, ''Anyone got an explanation for that? For the guy who knew he was going to get killed and then went out and got killed?''

''Probably did it to himself,'' said Jacobs. ''He was so sure that he was going to die that nothing he could do would change it. Walked into the ambush by being stupid. If he hadn't been so sure, he might not have done it.''

''Besides,'' said Tynan, ''we all know guys who said

they were going to die the next day and didn't. You only remember the ones who were right, for whatever reason, and forget all about the ones who were wrong.''

''It wasn't like that,'' protested Meyer. ''He knew. The others didn't give away everything they owned and didn't begin to make arrangements for their funerals.''

''I sometimes know things in advance,'' said Davis, quietly, almost as if he wasn't convinced of it himself.

''Oh, really,'' said Jacobs.

''Sometimes, I know that things are going to happen before they do. Just once in a while.''

''Then why don't you tell me who is going to win the World Series and I'll bet everything I own on it. Make a bundle in Vegas.''

''It doesn't work that way,'' said Davis.

''It never does,'' said Jacobs sarcastically. ''All you guys have a hundred excuses about why you can't predict something that'll make you all rich. Bullshit about ruining the gift by trying to capitalize on it.'' He shook his head in disbelief. ''What a pile of shit.''

''No,'' said Davis. ''What I mean is that I can't control it. If I could, I would be in Vegas playing roulette, picking the winning numbers every time. It comes in flashes. Things that I don't understand.''

''Like what?'' asked Jacobs.

Davis shrugged. ''The space shuttle Challenger is going to blow up. Explode, killing the whole crew, and everyone is going to see it happen on TV.''

''The space shuttle?'' said Jacobs. ''What in the hell is the space shuttle?''

''I don't know exactly,'' said Davis. ''I just know that it's going to be part of our space program in the future. After it explodes, there is going to be very little left of the space program.''

''When?'' asked Tynan.

"I don't know. I can just see some of the events around it and then a few afterward. I don't know when or anything else about it. Just a huge explosion in the middle of the morning and pieces of it begin raining out of a cloudless, blue sky, leaving trails of white smoke."

"What else?" asked Jacobs.

"We're not going to win in Vietnam."

"Now you're talking bullshit," said Jacobs. "There is no way that a third-rate, hell a fifth-rate, country can beat us in Vietnam."

"And you're right," said Davis, "except that they won't beat us. We'll negotiate a peace with them and a couple of years after we get our people out, they'll invade the south and we won't do a damned thing about it. We're going to let the news media and the college kids beat us."

"Okay," said Tynan, "I've heard enough of this bullshit now. I'm sorry, Davis, but I just don't believe this. You come up with a bunch of shit that can't be tested or examined and expect us to swallow it. Sometime in the future the Challenger will be destroyed, but you're not sure about it. You don't know what it is but it's going to happen."

"But it's true. I've seen it. And what about that woman in Washington, Jeane Dixon. She predicted the assassination of John Kennedy . . ."

"After the fact," said Tynan. "I saw nothing about it in print before the President was shot. And if I'm not mistaken, she also said the Russians would put the first men on the moon. That was wrong."

"Maybe not," said Davis. "Maybe their men were killed getting there so the Soviets just kept quiet about it. She never said they would be alive when they got there."

"Now you're splitting hairs," said Tynan. "She flat out blew that one."

Starkey returned with the Cokes and set them down on the table. "Come and get them."

Tynan grabbed one of the Cokes and pulled the pop-top free. He dropped it into an ashtray and took a deep drink. He set the can down and said, "It's going to take a lot more to convince me than some half-baked research into the subject. Especially when almost everyone seems to agree that there isn't much to the subject."

Sumner-Gleason returned then, saw the Cokes and shook his head. "Gentlemen, I thought that we had agreed that we wouldn't be violating our bodies with the various drugs and sugars that so readily abound in our world."

"Hell, I don't remember us agreeing to anything yet," said Jacobs. "Besides, Coke isn't a drug."

"Now that isn't exactly true. It contains caffeine, which is a mild drug."

"Found in nature," said Jacobs.

"Again true, but irrelevant. After today, gentlemen, we'll have to adhere to the diet, but I'm willing to compromise. One last night of unhealthful food and drink and then a proper diet. Now—"

"Before we get started," said Jacobs, "could I ask a question?"

"Sure," said Sumner-Gleason.

"Well, during the break, we were talking about some of this stuff, predictions of the future and the like, and I was wondering what you thought about it. Not the bullshit that you have to hand out in your lectures, but what you really thought about it."

Sumner-Gleason stepped up on the stage and leaned on the lecturn. He glanced to his left, out the windows and onto the parking lot. Finally he looked at the assembled men and said, "What I should tell you is that I believe in all this material. That I have researched it thoroughly and that I'm convinced there is something to this."

"But—" prompted Jacobs.

"But, I just don't know. The fakes and the charlatans

and the quacks have so saturated the field that it is hard to find anything that I can take seriously. I heard you mention Jeane Dixon, and there is good evidence that she did predict the assassination of Kennedy before it happened, but then she missed on Bobby Kennedy. Not a word about his death. Instead she said his political fortunes were on the decline. Too many of the predictions are vague so that they can be fit into almost any set of circumstances.''

"Then you don't believe," said Jacobs.

"That is not what I said. Besides, you've moved off the track. I'm here to enhance your capabilities for communication with one another and not for predicting the future. It's not really the same thing."

"Nice try," said Tynan, "but we're going to want an answer to the question and not a lot of fancy footwork."

"All right," said Sumner-Gleason. "I believe that the jury is still out on this. There is too much information about strange things for it to be completely discounted, and there do seem to be techniques for increasing the PSI potential in each of us. We'll try all that and see where it takes us, but I'm skeptical of the outcome."

"Then we're wasting our time," said Jacobs.

"Well, you're being paid for your time and we might learn a few things that will help you in the future, but I'm not expecting a great breakthrough here. We'll just roll with the punches and see where they take us."

"Great!" said Jacobs. "Just what I wanted to hear."

4

Bainbridge had no intention of returning to work after lunch. There were too many other things that he wanted to do, things that had to be done in person for them to have the necessary impact. Besides, no one would miss him, and since the police hadn't arrived, the woman obviously had kept her mouth shut.

He grinned as he thought about her return. A different blouse and skirt, her hair combed differently, and glasses instead of her contact lenses. She had worn a different coat to the office and hung it up next to the first one. She had glanced at him, and when she saw him watching, had looked away and hurried past.

For several minutes he waited to see what would happen, but she sat at her desk, cleaning up the mess that she had left there. Paper towels from the washroom to soak up the coffee that hadn't dried and then damp towels to scrub the rest. Papers ruined by the liquid were set to one side to be sorted out when they were dry.

When coworkers came over, she smiled at them, laughed with them, but stole glances at him. She made no move to go into the boss's office and the police never arrived. His threat had been effective. Maybe it was time to visit her at home and see how cooperative she could become.

At lunch he had waited for her but then had not spoken to her. He had wanted to see her face. There was a slight discoloring on her cheek, almost concealed by the heavy makeup she wore. She had rushed by him and he had felt like laughing at her.

After he had eaten, he drove to the underground parking lot just off lower Wacker Drive and circulated until he found the car he wanted. He sat there, waited until some-one else pulled out and then parked where he could watch the target vehicle. It belonged to a man just beginning to work his way up the Democratic Party machine. A small cog who, if he caught the right breaks, if he came to the attention of the right people, might one day be a major cog with a great deal of influence in Democratic politics. Bainbridge was investing in his own future by waiting for the rising star.

For the rest of the afternoon he sat there, waiting, sometimes listening to the radio, sometimes reading the paper, but waiting nonetheless. He watched the elevators at the far end of the garage and he watched the car that sat vacant. There were people coming and going, but none of them interested Bainbridge.

Finally, just after six, the door of the elevator opened and Bainbridge saw his victim. A young man in a light suit, white shirt and bright tie. His hair was fashionably long and he was accompanied by a young woman in a bright dress that ended short of her knees, boots and a waist-length coat. They were talking together, laughing, neither of them aware of the world around them.

Bainbridge opened his car door and moved to intercept them. He kept one hand in his pocket and searched the garage for signs that there were others around to hear. As he neared them, he said, "Mister Holbrook?"

The man stopped and turned toward him. "Yes?"

Bainbridge grinned and said, "I'd like a moment of your time, if you don't mind."

He flashed his teeth and said, "See my secretary for an appointment." He turned to go.

"I seriously doubt you want me to come to your office. That would leave a record."

"I'm very busy."

"This will take only a moment and then you can be on your way."

Holbrook looked at the woman with him and then handed her the keys. "I'll be there in a minute, Sara."

She shrugged, took the keys and headed toward the car. When she was out of earshot, Holbrook asked, "Now what is this all about?"

Bainbridge extracted the papers and held them up so that Holbrook could read them. As his eyes widened, Bainbridge took the first sheet off so that the second was visible.

"What do you want? Money?"

Bainbridge snorted once. "Money isn't going to do me any good. I have money and I can get more. I just want to be friends. Meet your friends, get introduced in the right places to make new friends."

"Ten thousand dollars and you give me those papers," said Holbrook.

"You can have them now, without money," said Bainbridge. "I have more. Copies of them."

"And if I don't give you what you want, they'll be published?"

"Of course. And a bright future will be ruined, something that neither of us wants. On the other hand, a little cooperation that won't hurt in the least, and I forget all about these papers."

Holbrook wiped a hand over his face, which was suddenly bathed in sweat. He could feel it dripping down his sides, turning his shirt clammy.

"One little indiscretion," said Holbrook.

"Except the lady complained to your superiors and you bought her off."

"She started it. It was all her idea, including taking the pictures. She even brought the camera. I had to do something about those damned pictures."

"You're unmarried and the pictures would be embarrassing, but you should have told her to go fish. Now it's too late. Anything you do is going to sink you. You've maneuvered yourself into a position from which you can't recover if this manages to reach the press."

"Unless I do business with you," said Holbrook.

There was the sound of a horn and Holbrook turned to see that Sara was growing impatient.

"You'd better make a decision and make it quickly."

"No money?" asked Holbrook.

"None. I just want a few introductions into the power structure. That's all. Nothing that is going to hurt you in any way. Then I forget all about the documents and you can go back to your mundane life."

"How do we handle this?"

Now Bainbridge grinned broadly. "I'll call you and you let me know what's going on. You refuse the call and your name will appear in the paper. You try to get even, you send muscle around, your name will appear in the paper. If you treat me right, no one has to know. Hell, it's not even morally wrong. I just want a little help."

The horn sounded again and Holbrook nodded. "Okay. You call me and I'll answer."

Holbrook hurried across the floor and got into the car parked there. He leaned to the right, kissed the woman and then the lights came on. They pulled out and drove toward the exit ramp.

"It's beginning," Bainbridge told himself. It had been so easy that he was wondering why he hadn't started six months earlier. Not that it mattered now, because he had started.

*   *   *

When the class was let out, about four, Tynan and Jacobs headed for the parking lot where they had left the car. Sumner-Gleason had told them that the nature of the class was classified and that they weren't to discuss the material outside of that room. Tynan realized that the reason for the classification was not because the information was secret but because the Navy didn't want to see a number of newspaper articles about training their men in ESP. Already under fire for trying to train dolphins to retrieve torpedos and for their somewhat haphazard investigations into unidentified flying objects, no one wanted more criticism about ESP.

But, as they got into the car and Jacobs started the engine, he asked, "What do you think of all this?"

Tynan leaned his head back and put a foot up on the dashboard. He then rolled down the window to cool the car's interior and said, "How in the hell should I know? It seems to me that the Navy wouldn't endorse something like this if there was nothing to it."

"But we have no way of knowing that. You know how the military tends to leap on fashionable bandwagons. This guy, Sumner-Gleason, might have sold them a bill of goods and there wasn't someone around with the balls or the brains to tell him to fuck off."

"Then we treat it like any other training we received during our Navy career. You pay attention in class, learn what you can and then use that which seems to be useful and forget about the rest."

Jacobs backed up and turned, pulling toward the street. He entered the traffic, slowed at the gate and then turned to the south along a tree-lined street with residential houses set well back. There were almost no people visible. It might have been because it was too hot in the afternoon sun, or that no one was around to be seen outside. Everyone was still at work or school or out shopping.

"So we just fuck around here, in Chicago, for two, three weeks and then go back to our units," said Jacobs as they slowed for a light.

"Better here than in the jungle practicing survival," said Tynan.

"I don't know. What about this diet thing that he's going to give us?"

Tynan shrugged as Jacobs started again. Tynan said, "Have a steak tonight, drink a beer and be prepared to live on slim rations for the next few days."

"Just like going into the jungle," said Jacobs. "Hey, you have plans for tonight?"

"Stevie and I will think of something."

"Oh, sure. I wasn't thinking." He stopped for another light, turned and then entered the motel parking lot. As he pulled up to the door, he said, "This is certainly better than being housed on base or living in the jungle."

"Anything would be better. See you tomorrow?"

"Pick you up about seven?"

"That's fine." Tynan watched the car pull away and then entered the motel. He walked down the hallway, a feeling of dread building in his gut. At first he attempted to dismiss it and then tried to focus on it, bring it to the surface. Had he been thinking about it, he would have realized that this was the kind of extrasensory perception that Sumner-Gleason had talked about during the afternoon. An unfocused feeling of impending doom that Tynan had learned to pay attention to. Something was not right and he was aware of it.

Earlier, before the first class, Tynan would have thought nothing of the feeling. He would have been alerted by it and assumed there was something wrong with his environment that his mind had detected but that his eyes and ears had missed. His unconscious mind was talking to him.

But then, he was in the hallway of a motel and there

should be no danger. He moved to the side so that one wall was close and moved along it until he reached the door to his room. He pulled the key from his pocket and glanced right and left. The hallway was empty.

He slipped the key into the lock and pushed the door open so that it bumped into the wall, proving that no one hid behind it. He entered, saw that the drapes were drawn, but a light near the bed burned. Then in the chair he saw King. She was wearing nearly nothing and pretending to read a magazine.

"You home, dear?" she asked.

Tynan nodded and then glanced to the right, into the bathroom, but no one hid there. As he moved deeper into the room, the feeling did not desert him, but then, it didn't intensify either. It was just there, a vague reminder that something bad was about to happen.

When he was sure that there was no one in the room other than King, he tossed his key into the middle of the bed and moved to her. She stood, displaying her body for him. Light from the lamp reflected off the smooth skin of her thighs and bare stomach. He wrapped his arms around her and kissed her deeply.

"You smell great," he whispered.

"Of course," she said. "Did you want to take your shower now?"

"You suggesting that I don't smell great? You suggesting that I need a shower?"

"No," she said, a smile on her face. "I just wondered if you wanted a chance to relax a little before . . ."

Tynan reached around and unhooked the wisp of material that was masquerading as a bra. She took it off and tossed it to the floor. Tynan used his hand, rubbing her chest lightly until he felt her nipples stiffen and harden. He bent slightly and kissed them. She purred deeply in her throat.

"What's the rush?" she asked.

"I missed you today. Had to sit in class and listen to lectures about a dozen boring things, and all I could think about was you."

King moved to the rear and sat down on the bed. She slipped up so that she was leaning against the headboard. She hooked her thumbs into the waistband of her panties and started to push them down, but then stopped, grinning wickedly.

Tynan sat down on the corner of the bed and studied her body as he had done many times before. He reached out and touched her leg, just above the knee, letting his fingers play against the soft skin on the inside of her thigh. He had been going to ask her what she knew about ESP, figuring that a social scientist versed in anthropology would know something about the subject, but then didn't. Other thoughts came to him.

King lifted her hips and slipped the waistband of her panties down, adjusting them so that they could be pulled off but so that they still covered her. She didn't speak.

Tynan moved then, letting his hand climb higher and higher on her leg. He touched her panties and realized that she was more than ready for him. She shuddered under his probing hand, her eyes closed and her head back.

"Now," she said.

Tynan stood up and stripped his shirt. He kept his eyes on her, watching the rise and fall of her chest as the breath came rapidly. Her hands were at her sides, clutching at the bedspread, balling the cloth in her fists.

"I've been thinking about you all day too," she said. "It's been so hard to concentrate."

Tynan sat down and took off his shoes, dropping them on the floor. He felt King reach around his waist and try to work the buckle on his pants, but the military buckle had been designed by the same people who had designed bra snaps. It was almost impossible for someone else to open. He pushed her hands out of the way and opened the buckle himself.

Again Tynan stood and kicked off his pants and took off his socks. He joined King on the bed, stretching out beside her, kissing her on the mouth and then the chin and throat and then working his way lower, lingering on her breasts and then on her belly button. King groaned and shifted and Tynan moved with her, the feeling of dread suddenly gone, pushed from his mind by other, more pressing thoughts.

Later, as they lay together, a light coating of sweat on them, an inner peace spreading through them, Tynan remembered his feeling. He probed for it, touched it and realized that it was still there, in the background, like a vulture waiting for something to die.

She rolled closer to him, her head on his chest, and asked, "What are you thinking about?"

He hesitated for only a moment and then said, "I was wondering what you knew about ESP."

5

Davis avoided the others until he got into the parking lot outside the classroom, and then he saw them again. Before he could duck back, they spotted him and waved him over.

"Going out to find something to eat and then downtown, into the city. You want to come along?" asked Harison.

"Nah," said the big man. "Thought I'd head on back to my room and catch some sleep."

"Women," said Meyer. "We are going in search of women. Young, able, willing women who hang around in bars drinking alcoholic beverages."

"Not tonight," said Davis. "Maybe tomorrow."

Meyer shrugged and said, "Tomorrow we won't be allowed to drink beer or eat real food and that fag instructor probably won't want us chasing women. It has to be tonight or we aren't going to have the opportunity."

Davis rubbed a hand over his face as if to wipe away sweat. He glanced up, into the late-afternoon sky, and said, "Well, tonight I'm tired and just want to head back to the motel. Maybe tomorrow."

"Suit yourself," said Meyer.

As the men climbed into a car, Davis walked over to the

rental vehicle that he had paid for himself. He didn't like being in a strange city without some kind of transportation. It limited him to the military base and his quarters. For a couple of bucks, he could rent a car and cure the problem. He didn't mind the money it cost him because the freedom it gave him was more than worth the cost.

He walked over to his car and unlocked the door. He turned and watched as Meyer, Harison and Starkey entered their vehicle. As they drove by, Harison raised a hand to wave at him and then they were out the gate. When they were out of sight, he climbed behind the wheel of his car, started it and then joined the line that was heading off base.

The trip to his motel was quick and within minutes he was in his room, out of uniform, relaxing in his underwear. In one hand he held a Coke and in the other, the *TV Guide*. Afternoon television was designed with the kids and their mothers in mind, except for WGN-TV, which had the Cubs playing again. Davis turned on the game, more for the background noise it would provide than for the entertainment value it held. The Cubs weren't doing much to entertain. The wind was blowing in.

As he watched, the images on the screen began to shimmer and shake and roll. For an instant he believed that the TV was broken and then realized that he was slipping from consciousness. The images of the players in baseball uniforms changed to men in military uniforms, black pajamas and web gear. They carried AK-47s instead of baseball bats. There weren't nine of them, but more like fifty of them, and the close-chopped grass of the manicured playing field changed to the rough, vegetation-choked fields of the Central Highlands, jungle that towered overhead and filled with wild life that called and screamed and fled. Water dripped and the light that could filtered down in bright rays that looked painted in the air.

Sweat born of heat and fear blossomed on his body, now clad in the tiger-striped fatigues that were not regulation issue. He had a band tied around his head to absorb the sweat and could feel the weight of his rucksack on his back. Cotton filled his mouth as he tried to breathe deeply and silently. The muscles of his thighs arched as he crouched in the jungle, hiding from the Viet Cong and North Vietnamese regulars. His fingers were wrapped around the stock of his weapon.

As the scene solidified around him and the motel room faded into the background, Davis knew that he was not dreaming or hallucinating. He was seeing into the future. His own future, which told him he would soon be back in Vietnam. Unlike the feelings of déjà vu that most people experienced, Davis had a full set of memories that he could draw on. He knew how he'd gotten there, and how long he would have to stay there. It was like walking into the middle of a movie that he had never seen, but one where he'd read the book. He knew what had happened up to that point, without having to experience the film, just as he knew what had led him to that particular portion of the jungle of South Vietnam.

The heat and humidity of the jungle was real. He felt the sweat drip and he felt the sickness caused by the heat. There was a lightheadedness that he tried to ignore as he watched the enemy slipping through the foliage. Without a sound or a word, he slid his hand along the stock of his weapon so that he could snap off the safety, moving it to the full-automatic position.

The pointman of the enemy unit halted for a moment, a patch of sunlight on his shoulder. He stared into the vegetation, as if suddenly aware of the Americans hiding behind it, but then started forward again. He wore a pith helmet and chest pouch that held spare magazines. The khaki of the pouch contrasted with the black of the silk pajamas. On his feet were sandals made from old truck tires.

Davis could see his face easily. A young man with a random pattern of long whiskers on his chin. He had a rounded face, brown eyes and jet-black hair. He was a short man, only an inch or two over five feet, and a thin man, probably not weighing more than a hundred pounds.

He walked on, past Davis, leading his patrol into the ambush. The main body appeared, worming its way through the dense jungle and out into the open area marked by the patch of sunlight. Davis froze, waiting for the blast that would signal the springing of the ambush.

Four days. Davis suddenly knew that he had been in the field four days and that when he got back to the ship he would be sent on R and R. He was a last-minute replacement for another man who had suddenly gotten sick. Vomiting and chills that suggested a serious illness and not goldbricking.

And then time seemed to stand still. The jungle fell silent, as if anticipating the coming battle. The explosion of the claymore mine ripped through the quiet just as the steel ballbearings ripped through the enemy's flesh. There were screams and cries and curses. M-16s began to hammer and the men in front of him began to dance. Bullets tore into them, causing them to jerk and twitch and fall to the ground. Blood spurted. Bodies, torn apart by the curtain of steel, collapsed.

Davis raised his weapon and opened fire on full auto. He swung the barrel along the line of the enemy's march. One man's head exploded and the body dropped. Another whirled, fell and rolled away. Firing from the enemy suddenly increased. Bullets were snapping through the jungle overhead. Leaves, bits of bark, splinters of wood began to rain down. Sound filled the air. There was the rattling of weapons. Explosions from grenades. Screams and shouts and orders. Noise rose and combined until it was almost a single, long detonation.

When his weapon was empty, Davis ducked and dropped the magazine to the jungle floor. He slammed another home and popped up, searching for a target. A round snapped by his head and Davis spun. He fired at a VC lying on the ground and saw the jungle floor erupt, the dirt splash almost like water in a rice paddy. The man rolled and returned fire, his weapon chattering like an angry monkey.

Davis aimed at the downed man and fired a single shot. Two rounds were short. Davis aimed higher and fired again. The man jerked once and rolled to his back. He reached upward, into the sky, and then collapsed. Blood spread from his wounds, soaking into the thick, green vegetation.

Firing increased around him, AKs on full auto, answering the M-16s. The chattering built and mingled and became one long explosion. There was a sudden burning in his shoulder. Davis felt the flaring heat burst outward, engulfing his whole chest, and knew that he had been hit. He dropped to the ground and rolled once. Somehow the noise had seemed to dim and the sun wasn't nearly as bright. He lost his weapon, having dropped it when the round hit him.

With his right hand he groped for his rifle, but couldn't find it. The sun seemed to have set and it was dark out. And then the sound faded completely.

Davis was confused by all this because his visions never ended that way, and suddenly he knew he had witnessed his own death in Vietnam, sometime in the future, sometime in the next year or so. Killed in an ambush that he and his fellow SEALS had set.

He sat in his motel room, transfixed by the images, or the lack of them, the fear building in him, clawing at his gut. Blackness of nonexistence, and then suddenly brightness, a glowing, white light that seemed to be like looking down a long tunnel. A calmness gripped him and he felt himself floating upward.

And then the vision faded.

Davis sat there, his T-shirt soaked with his sweat. The TV made a slight noise as the announcers called the Cubs baseball game. The Coke he had been holding was spilled on the carpet. Davis just couldn't move.

He knew the date and time that he was going to die. He knew it like he knew his own birth date. He would live to twenty-six years, seven months and twelve days. And then he would be killed in action by the Viet Cong in an undeclared war in Southeast Asia.

But there was no fear attached to the knowledge because he knew what would happen after he died. He had seen that too. He stood up and moved to the bathroom so that he could throw some cold water on his face. He glanced up into the mirror and saw that he was pale. Sweat was beaded on his forehead and his hair was plastered to the side of his head. Even the air-conditioning in the motel room couldn't dry it.

"Well, why not?" he asked out loud.

He returned to the main room and sat down in the chair. With the knowledge he now had, could he change the future? When it came time to go to Vietnam, he could refuse. They would throw him in jail, but then he wouldn't die in that ambush. Or, once in Vietnam, he could make sure that he didn't go on that patrol. Hell, that would be easy. He could arrange his R and R so that he wasn't around to participate, or he could be sick, or he could volunteer for something else before the patrol came up.

His knowledge was going to be his salvation. He could prevent his own death.

In all the time that he had been aware of his gift, he had never been in a position to make a change in the future. The events that he saw were so far removed from him that there was no way to prevent them. The death of the President wouldn't have been stopped by a letter sent to him. No matter how Davis had worded it, the President would still have gone to Dallas and the Secret Service would have assumed that Davis's warning was some kind of strange death threat, one of thousands they had to deal with. Nothing he said or did would have stopped the President from going to Dallas.

He stood up and moved to the television and slapped a hand against it, turning it off. He felt weak in the knees and sat down on the bed.

Never had he had the chance to change anything. He had known when playing cards if he should draw or if he should stand. He had known, sometimes, what cards the others held. He had known if he should fold or if he should play. But that wasn't the same as changing the future.

He sat there thinking about it and realized there was no question in his mind that he believed everything he had seen. It wasn't a question of some kind of strange hallucination. Each time he'd had a vision like that, it came true. Well, not every time, because some of the events had not happened, such as the end of the war in Vietnam.

Now, with only a little more than a year to live, he wondered if there was something else he should be doing, rather than letting the military run his life for the last few months. He should be out, living life to its fullest, because there was so little of it left.

He grinned and thought about the stories of terminally

ill patients who had run up huge bills, who had a good time, knowing that the companies would never be able to collect from them. He had no assets and his parents or girlfriend wouldn't be held responsible for his bills. The debts would die with him and the little money he had would be distributed among his creditors. Any claims would be filed against the estate which was next to nothing now.

But that was something he would think about in the future, tomorrow or the next day. He got off the bed and turned on the TV again. He saw that the Cubs were batting and then didn't care to watch the end of the game. He knew the Cubs would hold a lead until the top of the ninth, lose it, tie it up in the bottom of the inning and then win the game in the eleventh on a two-out home run with one man on. Knowing what would happen sure took the fun out of sports.

The funny thing was that it didn't always work. Most of the time he knew the outcome, but sometimes he didn't. It wasn't that he thought one team would win and then the other surprised him, it was that he didn't see a clear winner. That meant there must be other factors that hadn't come into play. Someone could change the outcome by a super effort and somehow that effort had not been determined by the fates or by God or by whatever controlled the outcome of the game.

Davis shrugged and got up off the bed. He moved to his suitcase and picked up his clothes. He put them on and forced all the thoughts of ESP, precognition and the future from his mind. He would go to the motel's restaurant, have dinner and return to watch television.

Tomorrow, he would listen to what Sumner-Gleason had to say and he would talk to the lieutenant, tell him some of what he knew and see if he could come up with a plan to save his life. Then he'd have to concentrate on the latest vision because they usually came at random. He'd have to learn to control the ability better so that he could check on his progress in saving his own life.

But that was for tomorrow. Now there was dinner to get through. And the night. For some reason he felt that it was going to be a long night.

6

The class the next day started with another lecture. Sumner-Gleason again reviewed the progress that had been made in paranormal studies. He ignored the ghost stories and the demonologists and stuck with the investigations of ESP. He talked about Rhine again and then displayed a series of five cards, each with a symbol on it. There was a square, wavey lines, a star, a circle and a cross. A person with no esper ability, by sheer chance, should guess between twelve and twenty right for every hundred shown. Those experiments had been carried out over a period of years by others. The results were now a standard used to gauge the ability of new subjects.

"So, before we launch into the training sessions, I want to conduct a test to determine if any of you possess a latent talent," he said finishing the lecture. He stood there and grinned at them.

"And then?" asked Tynan.

"And then we'll begin a study session and, at the end, take the tests again to determine if there has been any improvement in the scores. We need to build a file on each of you as a control. Now, who wants to go first?"

No one said a word. Everyone suddenly found something interesting to study. Tynan wanted to watch the people outside. Jacobs was cleaning his fingernails. Davis and Harison were reading the course syllabus and the last two men were looking at the back wall.

"It's not that big a deal," said Sumner-Gleason. "Lieutenant, why don't you go first. Show the men that this isn't anything dangerous."

Tynan shrugged. "Sure." He stood up and waited for the instructor.

Sumner-Gleason picked up his cards and a clipboard. He started for the door, stopped and said, "We'll want to have a little privacy."

Tynan followed the man out. They walked down the hall and entered a small office. Inside there was a single table that had a partition in the center so that it looked like a ping-pong table with a very high, opaque net. There were chairs at either end of the table. A fluorescent light hung from the ceiling. The walls were painted a light gray and there were no pictures on it. There was nothing in the room to distract either the subject or the researcher.

"Have a seat," said Sumner-Gleason.

Tynan pulled out the chair and sat. He stared at the partition made of plywood and painted a sickening color of green. The paint had been spread on it so thick that it was impossible to see the grain of the wood. It was a solid, blank wall.

Sumner-Gleason sat down on the other side of the wall. He raised his voice, although it wasn't necessary. "We'll go through this two times. First time through, I won't say anything to you except 'Next.' You'll have no idea how you did. Second time through, I'm going to tell you if you were right or wrong. See if positive reinforcement, even as limited as that, improves your score significantly. Now, any questions?"

Tynan folded his hands and stared at the top of the table. "Just one. You really believe in this?"

"I don't disbelieve," said Sumner-Gleason. "I keep an open mind and see where it leads. I conduct experiments to learn more about it. If you're ready . . ."

"Go ahead."

They started then. Tynan concentrated, trying to figure out which card Sumner-Gleason was holding. At first there was nothing there and he guessed. Later an image would form in his mind, an impression, and he would guess that symbol. Sometimes there wouldn't be much and Tynan would pick at it, trying to figure out which card. As they progressed through the session, Tynan realized that the first impression, the one he sometimes resisted, was the one he should be using. Forget everything else, just take the first image and use it.

When they had gotten through all one hundred, Sumner-Gleason said, "That's it."

"How'd I do?"

There was a moment of silence and then he said, "I make it nineteen right, though most of those were toward the end of the run."

"That significant?"

"Not at all. Too many misses for it to be significant. If you're ready, we'll start the second run."

"Go ahead."

Again they started and Tynan followed the plan he had developed with the first group. If he received any kind of impression, that was what he said. He didn't concentrate on trying to figure something out. He tried to open his mind, to make it receptive.

And as they went through the cards, it seemed that Sumner-Gleason was saying "Right" more often than not. He seemed to be getting better. When the test ended, he sat patiently, waiting for the other man to make a count.

"What'd you do differently, Lieutenant?"

Tynan grinned and told him.

"Your score is better, though it's not earth-shattering. Better than statistical probability. You might have a latent talent there that can be developed."

"So what happens now?"

"I test one of the other men and you can go back to the classroom. Then, just before lunch, we'll discuss the diet plans and a couple of simple exercises that might help to improve any talent you have."

"I meant what do I do now?"

"Nothing. We just continue the testing and then, if there are any kind of positive results from the others, we can form a plan. If there isn't, then we may have to devise another strategy."

Thinking about the discussion that the men had held the day before, while Sumner-Gleason was out of the room, Tynan asked, "What do you think about precognition? About predicting the future?"

"I think that I have never seen any good evidence that it can be done."

Tynan slid back his chair and put his feet up on the table to relax. "I remember that a mind reader came to town about three weeks before his show, sealed a piece of paper in an envelope and said that he'd written down the head-line of the local paper for the day he'd be back."

"And when they opened it, the headline was there," finished Sumner-Gleason.

"Not exact, but close. How'd he know if there isn't any precognition?"

"Simple sleight of hand. If someone else opened the envelope before the magician touched it, I'd be impressed, but I'll bet dollars to donuts that the man had some excuse to hold that envelope before it was opened, maybe claim-ing that he wanted to make sure it was the same envelope they had sealed up earlier. If he touched it, he switched. It's one of the oldest tricks."

"Shit, I thought it was a good one. I mean, I thought there'd be no way to do that if he couldn't really predict the future."

Sumner-Gleason stood up and walked around the partition. He sat on the edge of the table, his clipboard in one hand. "Let me tell you a little story. I saw a man on TV who claimed to have psychic powers, said that he could bend spoons with his mind. He wouldn't do it in the laboratory where slow-motion cameras could record everything, but he would do it on national television. Hell, it was an impressive demonstration. He bent spoons, forks, keys, a whole host of things."

"Proving that he had a power," said Tynan.

"Then," said Sumner-Gleason, ignoring Tynan's words, "a stage magician came on and said there was nothing to it. He'd use his powers and repeat the trick. He bent spoons, forks, keys, everything. But before the host could speak, the man declared it was a trick and that no psychic power had been involved. If you knew how to do it, it was simple."

"What'd the psychic say?"

"Denied that it was a trick. Admitted that the magician could do it. Hell, the man had done it, but also said that he, the psychic, was using no trickery, though the magician obviously was."

"Stalemate," said Tynan.

"No, the magician finally won. He suggested that if it was mental power that bent the spoons, there was no reason it couldn't be done in the lab where scientists could watch and cameras could record. That would prove there was no trick once and for all."

"What'd the psychic say?"

Sumner-Gleason snorted. "Claimed that surrounded by all that skepticism, he wouldn't be able to perform. Too much negative energy."

Now Tynan nodded. "So much bullshit because the cameras were sure to catch him faking it."

"Exactly."

Davis, the next test subject, entered the room and took a seat. Sumner-Gleason explained the procedure to him, and before they even started, he saw a parade of the cards in front of him. Not only could he see the cards, but he could predict the order in which they would appear.

He sat there, waiting as Sumner-Gleason droned on and on, telling him about the test. Davis already knew about it. In high school he had read up on the subject, trying to learn how unusual his gift was.

But then they were into the test and Davis was concentrating on the cards, on the stars and squares and wavy lines, until the partition in front of him began to shimmer and glow and faded away. No longer was he seeing the cards and the walls and the room; he was looking off into another high-tech room filled with computer screens and glowing images. There were bright maps and blinking warning lights. There was a small man standing near one of the consoles, giving orders. The dark hair was sprinkled with gray, as was his neatly trimmed beard. He had bright eyes, glowing with anticipation, a single eyebrow and a pointed chin. There was an intense look on his face. It was obvious that he was in charge and that he was important. Three men in business suits stood close to him, and right behind them were six military officers.

Davis didn't recognize the room and he didn't understand the importance of all the computers. But then he knew he was watching the War Room at the Pentagon and that the world situation had deteriorated to the point where the nuclear holocaust was only hours away.

The man surrounded by his aides and bodyguards was the President of the United States. A man who had not been elected to the office but appointed to the presidential cabinent. When a terrorist bomb four weeks earlier had killed the President, Vice President and the Speaker of the House, the man had risen to the top. The natural order of selection had been voted down because the President Pro Tem of the Senate was gravely ill and expected to die soon. And the fact that he belonged to the other party hadn't helped.

As he watched the scene, Davis knew that the man had engineered everything except the illness of the President Pro Tem. That had been a convenient coincidence. Everything had come together for a man who had planned and connived and blackmailed his way to the top in the administration. Now he stood in command of a military force with the power to destroy the world a dozen times over. And he was a man who would not hesitate to use that power.

The faces of the people in the room, many of them lighted by only the glow from the computer screens, were full of fear. A few of the women were openly crying; one man was shaking with fear. All knew that the world, as they knew it, was going to cease to exist in a very few hours. Families, friends, neighbors were about to die in a flash of light and fire. The towns, cities, farms, everything were going to be turned into ruins. The fear was almost visible.

Davis could pick out snippets of conversation: the President conferring with his advisors, intelligence officers talking about the state of readiness of the Soviet forces. But then something he didn't understand: the enemy in the coming war was not the Soviets but someone in the Middle East. A rogue power with a few missiles and nuclear warheads. It made no difference that the enemy had only a few weapons and no delivery system. The war would escalate until the Soviets and the Americans were trying to destroy each other.

"Mister Davis," said Sumner-Gleason, his voice unnaturally loud. "Do you see the shape on this card?"

Davis didn't hear the words. He was watching as the President grinned and said, "Don't give them the chance. Hit them first."

"We don't have the capability for a preemptive strike," said one of the military officers.

"We can do enough to them to limit the damage they do to us. We can take out enough of their weapons so their retaliatory capability is reduced."

"Providing those weapons are still on the ground when ours hit," said one of the generals. "If they launch on detection, then their weapons will be airborne, and they can get their whole missile fleet into the air before one of ours hits any of their silos."

The President slammed a fist onto the top of a computer console, cracking the screen. There was a flash, a popping and a shower of sparks. He glared at the man who had spoken and demanded, "Who do you think you're talking to?"

The officer remained mute.

"You will take my orders and execute them. If you fail, then it is you who will be executed."

"Yes, sir."

The President turned and Davis got a good look at his face, a face filled with hate and rage. Davis knew that he wouldn't forget what the man looked like. Not ever.

"President Bainbridge," said one of the women sitting at a console, "I have a launch detection."

And then the vision faded. Gone in a flash, replaced by a card with a star in the center of it.

"Mister Davis, do you see the card?" asked Sumner-Gleason again. Then he asked, "Are you all right?"

"Star," said Davis, his voice low, husky. He was drenched in sweat, his body clammy from it. He felt lightheaded, sickened. A President named Bainbridge was going to destroy the world, tear down civilization in a demented attempt to control the world, in a demented attempt to rule Supreme.

"And now?" asked Sumner-Gleason prompting him.

"Circle."

He wiped the sweat from his face. There was a hollow feeling in his gut and there were chills running up and down his spine. He felt as if he'd just done a hundred pushups or hiked twenty miles with a hundred pounds on his back. He was exhausted and panicked and sickened.

The germ of an idea came to him then. Not a fully developed idea but one that he could act on. He would have to learn whether or not he could change the future. He had the information he needed to do it. He knew the man's name and then suddenly he knew that the man was in Chicago with him, working downtown but already beginning to make his first moves, moves that would take him to the President's office.

"Mister Davis, are you concentrating?"

"Star again. And next will be the wavy lines."

He sat forward and leaned his forehead on his arms. He closed his eyes and wondered if he should try to find Bainbridge. Talking would do no good. The man would laugh at attempts to talk him out of the course that would lead to the White House. It would be like trying to talk an armed robber out of robbing you. He wouldn't listen and the only way to stop him would be to take action.

"Are you all right?" asked Sumner-Gleason again.

Davis opened his eyes and lifted his head. He stared at the instructor and said, "I'm fine."

"You didn't miss any until you stopped talking."

"I know," said Davis. "I've always been very good at guessing games."

"It's more than that."

"Of course. I know it and now you know it," Davis looked as if there was more that he wanted to say but didn't. He fell silent.

"I'm going to want to explore this further. Can you do this all the time?"

"Yes, sir. Most of it."

"Is there something wrong now?"

Davis almost blurted out what he had seen, but then didn't. Sumner-Gleason might understand the mechanics of ESP and precognition, but he was a civilian. That meant that he was someone who couldn't be completely trusted. He was an outsider who understood nothing of the military mind.

"It's hard," he said. "The concentration is hard, and you wanted to continue for so long."

"Uh-huh," said Sumner-Gleason. "So this isn't something that you can do all the time."

"I can do it anytime," snapped Davis, "but I don't like to. It makes my head hurt."

Sumner-Gleason pulled a handkerchief from his pocket and mopped his face with it. There were things that he wanted to say but knew that he didn't have to hurry. Davis would be around for another three weeks, and if things went as well as they were now, Sumner-Gleason was sure the Navy would let him continue. He would have to be patient; that was the key to the whole thing. To Davis, he said, "That's all I have for now."

"Then I can go?"

"Yes, but please don't mention your success to the others just yet. I don't want to adversely influence their results."

"Yes, sir."

Davis opened the door and stepped into the hallway. Once out of the room, he felt like collapsing. So much was coming at him so quickly now. Yesterday the Vietnam episode and today the end of the world. So much to understand, so much for him to do, and yet there was never any doubt in his mind. He knew that a man named Bainbridge would one day, twenty-five years in the future, launch an atomic war.

"But can I do anything about it?" he asked himself out loud. And then he wondered, Should I?

7

Bainbridge stood in the boss's office, staring at the desk and wondering how the woman had had the courage to inform on him. He knew that he was in trouble because he hadn't been asked to sit down, yet. Instead, he stood there, on the light blue carpeting, watching his boss, William P. Smith, who read from a typed sheet.

Smith was a heavy man, almost fat. He had a round face and a receding hairline. There were beads of sweat on his face. He sat there, in shirt sleeves, sweat stains under his arms. His tie was loosened and he hadn't spoken except to tell Bainbridge to stand there.

The woman, a handkerchief clutched in her hand, sat in one of the four chairs that lined the wall. She had her head bowed so that he couldn't see her face. She wore a short skirt, a light blouse and high-heeled shoes. It was obvious that she was crying about the confrontation.

"All right, Jason, what do you have to say for yourself?" asked Smith.

Bainbridge almost laughed. This was all so stupid. He decided to bluff his way through it. No one was going to believe a woman who sat in the corner and cried almost hysterically.

"Say about what?" he asked innocently.

"Rachel here," Smith said flipping a hand in her direction, "claims that you hit her yesterday morning. Bloodied her nose and hurt her."

Bainbridge shot her a glance and then looked back at Smith. "I'm supposed to deny this?"

"You're supposed to tell me the truth. There is no room in this business for this kind of employee infighting." Smith wiped his face again and added hastily. "When you leave here, only one of you will still have a job."

"That's not fair," said Rachel. "You can't fire me."

Smith looked at her and said, "Young woman, I will not dismiss Mr. Bainbridge on your word alone. That would be exceedingly unfair. I will hear both sides of the story before I make a decision."

"There is no story," said Bainbridge. "I don't know what she's talking about. I don't have the faintest idea of what's going on here."

Smith consulted his notes and said, "Rachel has accused you of striking her yesterday. Of trying to force your affections on her, and when she rejected you, you struck her in the face, bloodying her nose."

Now Bainbridge did laugh. It was a laugh without mirth, without humor. "I still don't know what she's talking about. Do I look like the kind of man who would strike a woman or try to force myself on her?"

"You were angry," she said, her voice rising.

"This was yesterday? Then where was everyone?" asked Bainbridge.

"A good question," said Smith.

"It was early, before they arrived."

"Oh," said Bainbridge, his voice holding a slightly mocking note. "You sat here yesterday and no one noticed that your nose was bleeding?"

"I went home and changed," she said. "You know that. You saw me go."

Bainbridge turned and said, "Do I have to stand here and listen to this? She is obviously lying, though I can't think of why she would want to lie."

"I'm not lying. You are." She stared at him, her face a mask of rage. "I'm not going to let you get away with this."

"Mr. Smith," said Bainbridge, "I have work to do and I don't see the point in listening to these lies. The woman has an ax to grind. Maybe it's because I never asked her out for a drink."

"I wouldn't go out with you if you were the last man alive on the planet."

Bainbridge shrugged but didn't respond. He had manipulated her into losing her temper, undercutting her own arguments. He knew that his best course was to stand there quietly, respectfully, and let Rachel destroy herself.

She was on her feet, now leaning over Smith's desk. Her eyes were red from crying. "You can't let him do this. He struck me and threatened me."

Smith looked from her face to Bainbridge and then back again. Finally he said, "Jason, you can go. I'll speak to you again this afternoon."

"Are you sure, sir?"

"Of course. Go on back to your desk. You're doing a fine job for us."

"No!" yelled Rachel. "No!"

"I think it would be best for everyone if you cleaned out your desk today. We'll give you a week's severance pay, but I'm afraid that we won't be able to give you a positive recommendation."

"That's not fair," she said.

"It's more than fair. You come in here with an unsubstantiated story and make demands that I fire a valued, hard-working employee. He's done nothing to indicate that he hit you or has even talked to you."

Bainbridge moved rapidly to the door and then closed it on his way out. He heard Rachel's voice once but couldn't tell what she was saying.

At his desk, he sat there grinning to himself. It was the calm facade and the ability to lie easily and convincingly. People just didn't understand the nature of lying. Adolph Hitler had said that if you tell a lie often enough, people would believe it. And the bigger the lie, the more likely they would believe it.

A moment later Smith's door slammed. Rachel stomped out, her back rigid. She marched to her desk, jerked open a drawer and began pawing through it. She tossed everything that belonged to the company on the floor.

Two other women moved toward her, but she spun on them with such fury that they stopped dead in their tracks. They glanced at one another, unsure of what to do, and then retreated, leaving Rachel alone.

Bainbridge sat down again and then watched the door, waiting for her. As she left the building for the last time, he moved to intercept her. She stopped when he spoke to him, focusing all the anger on him.

"I told you what would happen," he said quietly. "You wouldn't listen. A piece of advice, next time you go after someone, maintain your cool, have all the facts lined up on your side, and . . ." He stopped talking, looked around to see that no one was near them to hear his last bit of advice. "And lie through your teeth."

"Fuck you!" was all that she said.

Sumner-Gleason had a hard time concentrating on the rest of the tests. He had never deluded himself. He knew that he was not gifted in PSI talent but felt that he needed to concentrate on the task if the subject was going to have a chance to determine the symbol on the card. It was his belief that those with high esper ratings during the simple test picked up their indications of the symbols by reading the mind of the sender. It hadn't occurred to him to turn the cards face down on the table and point to them.

So now, with Harison in the room with him, trying, with no success, to guess which card was being held, Sumner-Gleason felt his mind wandering. Never, but never in the seven years that he had been involved in psychic research, had he found a subject like Davis. He had never seen anyone score a hundred percent on the test. Seventy-five percent, eighty percent, but never a hundred percent.

Harison, on the other hand, was scoring so poorly, it was almost as if he could read the cards and then picked any of the other four symbols. Rarely had anyone scored so poorly, and Sumner-Gleason wondered if it had anything to do with his lack of concentration.

He hurried through the tests, thanked Harison and then called a halt for the morning. He could take it no longer. As soon as he had let everyone go for lunch, he rushed back to his office and picked up the phone.

"Dr. Bannon, Sumner-Gleason here."

"Yes, Harlan, what can I do for you?"

"I've had some startling results on the preliminary phase of the initial tests. A subject who was able to ascertain the correct symbol every time."

"No opportunity for a trickster?"

"I wouldn't see how. I controlled all the conditions of the test. I selected the facility and the subject wasn't aware that the tests were going to be held. The preliminary results are quite exciting."

"Yes, Harlan, they sound exciting." Except that Bannon's voice didn't convey any excitement. "What is your next move there?"

"Obviously, I must determine if the subject can repeat the performance. It might have been a fluke, though I doubt it. I believe his scores are going to be consistent."

"Belief is not a word that I like hearing in a scientific conversation," Bannon cautioned.

"Of course not," agreed Sumner-Gleason. "However, without making the tests, I must speculate on the already-observed data. That speculation suggests that the subject's scores will remain consistent."

"A long-winded way of saying the same thing though more acceptable."

"Yes."

"Will you be bringing the subject here for further testing?"

"That may not be as simple as it seems," said Sumner-Gleason. "I don't believe he is comfortable with his gift and therefore will resist our attempts at further study."

"That sort of an attitude makes me suspicious," said Bannon.

"And me; however, I will do what I can. If he continues to perform at this high level, I think that we might have the beginnings of an important paper."

"Don't let your expectations run wild, Doctor," cautioned Bannon again. "This is a very preliminary stage and we've seen other subjects who have performed almost as well faulter as the tests became increasingly difficult."

"Yes, I know. Anyway, I just wanted to advise you of the situation here."

"Thank you. Good-bye."

"Good-bye," said Sumner-Gleason. He hung up slowly and then sat staring at the phone. Not exactly what he had expected with the call, but then Bannon was probably jealous of his discovery. With Davis, it would be possible to prove that certain forms of ESP did exist. Davis was a very rare person. Someone who had no reason to show off, a man who hadn't tried to exploit his gift, a man who had not sought them out. By carefully handling the case, he would be able to demonstrate, in the laboratory, over and over, that there was such a thing as ESP. Men who had postulated theories with less success were widely known in the field. Sumner-Gleason would be able to prove their theories and see his name rise to the top.

He got up and left the tiny office, wondering exactly what he should do. The excitement of the discovery was coursing through him. He wanted to run or shout or scream but didn't. Instead, he slowly walked down the hallway, telling himself to remain calm.

But he felt a pressure to do something, to do something immediately. If he didn't act right away, the discovery would somehow get away from him. It was a feeling that he couldn't explain. It was the kind of feeling that he normally ignored and was the closest that he would ever come to experiencing the psychic phenomena personally.

The SEALS sat in the classroom, shooting the shit. Tynan was relaxing in one corner, looking out the window and wishing that he had brought something to read. He'd been involved in enough military classes to know that they sometimes didn't get going on time. Everyone was expected to be there promptly, ready to learn, but then the instructor would be someplace else, doing something else, so that ten, fifteen, twenty men would be standing around restless and bored.

He remembered one mandatory class, driven by the civilian-world perception of the military. Everyone was going to be taught something about human relations. They had to be there at eight in the morning. Tynan, with thirty other men, arrived on time, but the instructor hadn't gotten there until an hour later. He'd gotten the time wrong, so thirty sailors sat around with nothing to do, wasting the taxpayer's money.

This was the same thing, with Sumner-Gleason off trying to learn who had psychic ability and who didn't. The rest of them sat there with nothing to do but wait for the return of the instructor.

As he watched a civilian woman walking across the parking lot, a woman dressed in as little as she could possibly wear and not be arrested, Davis sat down next to him.

"Sir, can I talk to you for a moment?"

"Sure. What's on your mind?" Tynan hadn't taken his eyes off the woman, who had stopped walking and seemed to be waiting for someone.

Davis didn't speak again right away. He followed Tynan's gaze and saw the woman. She waved at someone and then hurried from sight.

"Sir, it's a personal matter. Something that I'd rather not discuss here, in the classroom."

"Maybe you should wait until you get back to your own unit then."

"No, sir, it's something that has to be taken care of here, while I'm able to do it."

Tynan looked at his watch and saw that they would be breaking for the day in a few minutes and said, "Why don't we talk about it during dinner. I'll get the car from Jacobs and you and I'll go find something to eat."

"That would be fine, if you don't mind, sir."

"Meet me in the parking lot then."

"Yes, sir."

As Davis left, Jacobs slipped into the chair that he had vacated. "What was that all about?"

Tynan shrugged. "Seems he has a problem that he wants to discuss with me. I don't know what it is."

Jacobs glanced at Davis and then looked back to Tynan. "Maybe he got his girl pregnant."

"That a major problem in today's society? That something you couldn't handle yourself?"

"I guess not."

"Then give me the keys and let me have the car. I'll find out about it later."

"How am I supposed to get around tonight?"

Tynan grinned. "You'll just have to rely on your friends over there. I'll pick you up in the morning. You'll get to sleep late that way."

"Yes, sir." He pulled the keys from his pocket and then grinned. "Make sure you fill it before you return it."

"You mean that we don't get to use the base POL?"

"Oh yes, sir. They'll fill it at the motor pool, if you drive it over there. It's just that you have to hassle with everyone to get it filled because no one wants to help you get it done."

"Fine," said Tynan. "Happy to do it."

Jacobs looked at his watch and said, "It time for us to get out of here?"

"Close enough," said Tynan. "If Sumner-Gleason wanted us to hang around after sixteen hundred, he should have said something." Tynan stood and raised his voice. "That's it, gentlemen. Let's cut out and be back here at zero eight hundred."

8

Tynan had suggested that they pick up King so that she could eat with them, but Davis had refused. He told the lieutenant that it was something personal, and once Tynan knew the whole story, then he might not want to have King involved.

Davis was nervous. The only thing that he really knew about Tynan was that he had gone through the same training, gone to the same school where the huge sign dominates all, including their lives: THE ONLY EASY DAY WAS YESTERDAY. Tynan had been through it all, and that made him someone to be trusted, if only because of the black beret and the special insignia that they sometimes wore. A man who wouldn't doubt his word, no matter how far out the discussion went, because under it all, they were brothers.

As they drove through the residential area that surrounded the air station, Davis tried to figure out how much he should say and how much he should hold back. The others had joked about his predictions of the future but it had been good natured in a classroom where everyone tended to exaggerate. Now he was about to take it farther.

They stopped outside a brick building that had few windows and a door made of smoked glass. There weren't many cars in the lot because it was fairly early to be getting dinner. Another hour would signal the beginning of the dinner rush.

"This look good to you?" asked Tynan.

"Looks just fine, sir."

Tynan got out, locked his door and watched as Davis did the same. Davis got the door and they entered. Inside it was cool and dark. There was quiet music coming from a jukebox stuffed into a corner. Around the walls were booths with high backs that would provide some privacy. There were tables with checkered table clothes and glowing candles on them. It was a nice, quiet, relaxed place.

"Take the one that suits you," said Tynan.

Davis moved as far from the door as he could get, taking in the rear a corner booth that was partially shielded by potted plants hanging from the ceiling. One great fern had thick branches that reached to the floor.

As they sat down, Tynan asked, "You want to eat or just a beer?"

"Beer would be fine."

A waitress, dressed in a red uniform with white trim, appeared, took their order and then vanished. A moment later she was back with a pitcher and two frosted mugs. Tynan poured, took a deep drink and then said, "Okay, what's on your mind?"

"You don't beat around the bush, do you, sir?"

Tynan set his mug down and leaned back. He closed his eyes for a moment and then said, "I have, waiting for me at the motel, a beautiful, intelligent young woman. She is waiting for me to take her out. Now, I'm as sociable as the next man, but you don't hold a candle to her."

Davis smiled. "I understand." He fell silent, studied the pattern of the table cloth and said, "You went through Coronado. You went for the swims and the runs and the exercises and came back bone tired and covered with mud and shit. You went through all that, just as I did.''

"Yes,'' agreed Tynan.

"You know what a man has to do to get through that. You know that the hustlers, the fakers, the macho types, the bullshit artists don't last very long.''

"Agreed,'' said Tynan, nodding.

"Those of us who make it have something in common. You might say that we're all something special.''

Tynan picked up his beer and drank. As he set it down, he asked, "There a point to all this?''

"Yes, sir, there is,'' said Davis. He picked up his glass and drank half the beer in a single, massive gulp. He belched once, wiped his lips with his napkin and then began to speak again. "You remember yesterday that I . . .''

And then he stopped. Somehow what he had been going to say was not exactly what he wanted to say. It would leave everything out in the open, for Tynan to see and reject without an opportunity to hear all the evidence. To hear what was coming to the forefront.

"Let me change that,'' said Davis. "I want to talk about something that's related to the main issue but is going to sound like it's out of left field.''

Tynan didn't answer him immediately. He watched the waitress come at them again. With so few people in the place at the moment, she wanted to get them served while it was easy. Tynan waved her off and then said, "Go ahead, remembering that I have a lady waiting.''

"Then let me ask you this. If you had been in a position to know what Adoph Hitler was going to do before he did it, would you have shot him?''

Tynan grinned and then picked up his beer, draining the mug. "My gut reaction is to say, 'Of course.' But then I think about everything else. How would I know for sure? Who am I to judge this man before he ever commits any of the outrages that he commited? By the time you could see the direction that he was going, it was too late.''

"Let's say that you knew. Let's say that there was no doubt that if he lived, he would plunge the world into war and that he would kill, literally, millions. That he would start a world war. Would you shoot him?''

"This is an idle exercise,'' said Tynan.

"Yes, sir.''

For a moment they sat in silence. Tynan watched Davis, who was staring now at the bubbles in the beer. He was watching that with such an intensity, that Tynan was no longer sure that Davis knew where he was.

To break the mood, Tynan said, "I suppose that if I knew what Hitler was going to do, I might be inclined to try to stop him. The problem is that we don't know if he was the worst one to have in the position he held. You have to admit that toward the end there, he was one of the best things we had working for us. His demented ideas and ridiculous plans cost him the war. His mistakes saved thousands of allied lives.''

"What do you mean?''

Tynan shrugged. "Hitler kind of got the ball rolling. He put together everything. The man was a genius in that respect. But then, toward the end, he started making decisions that weren't the best for Germany. The Sixth Army, I believe, was surrounded in Stalingrad. The commander wanted to retreat but instead Hitler made him a field marshal, telling him that a German field marshal had never been captured. It threw away an entire German army. Someone else might have told the commander to retreat and consolidate.''

"Then you're saying that you wouldn't shoot Hitler.''

Tynan poured himself another beer and watched as the head built and foam dripped down the outside of the glass. He wasn't sure he wanted to go on with the discussion. It had taken a decidedly strange turn and he wasn't sure that he wanted to continue. Off-duty hours were supposed to be for fun, not deep philosophical discussions.

Finally Tynan said, "I really don't know. It would depend on so much. I'd have to believe that ridding the world of him would be the thing to do, but you're talking about playing God. Suddenly you're the judge, jury and executioner."

"But look what he did."

"Yes, now," said Tynan, "with hindsight, knowing, I wouldn't have any regrets. I'd pull the trigger. But put me into 1928 or 1930 and I just don't know."

"If you'd seen what was going to happen, you wouldn't pull the trigger?"

Tynan felt his head begin to spin. He could see exactly what Davis was asking. If he knew that he could prevent the horror of World War II would he do it. The answer had to be yes. There was nothing else it could be.

"Yes, I'd pull the trigger. It's that doubt that would be in my mind and there would never be any way to find out if you were right or wrong. Once the trigger was pulled, history would, or rather the future would change. Maybe Hitler would become a national hero and the German army would sweep over Europe anyway. Maybe they would view the death of their leader as the first round in the beginning of the war so that it started no matter what had been done. Who knows what the result would be."

"I would think," said Davis, "that you'd have to pull the trigger. There is no way to work around it."

"This leading someplace?" asked Tynan.

Davis shrugged, unsure of what to do or what to say. The conversation hadn't gone in the direction that he had expected it to. Now, it would be impossible for him to blurt out the real reason for his questions. Tynan wouldn't understand. Hell, there wasn't anyone in the world who would understand. Who could understand.

To cover his confusion, Davis poured himself the last of the beer. He drank some of it and then asked, "What do you think of all this ESP stuff that we're being hit with?"

"I think that it is a big waste of our valuable time," snapped Tynan.

"Then you don't believe in it?" asked Davis.

Tynan shook his head and said, "Did I say that? I just don't think that it's something they can teach us. And I don't see how it's going to be helpful."

"You still don't believe that I can, sometimes, predict the future?"

Tynan stared at the man and asked, "Is that what this is about? I'm sorry, but no, I don't believe it. I do believe that there are things happening that none of us can explain, and I'm not calling you a liar, but until I see some proof of what you claim, I can't accept it."

Davis nodded. "Fair enough."

"I hope that I haven't insulted you with my attitude," said Tynan, "but you have to look at it from my point of view. Until I have some proof, there is no reason for me to believe that you can predict the future."

"No, sir. None at all." Davis finished his beer and wondered how it had gone so wrong. He had thought that Tynan would listen to him and accept his story, if only because it came from a fellow SEAL. Maybe the bond wasn't as strong as he had thought it was.

And then he realized he wasn't being fair. He'd hit the lieutenant with so much that was so strange that it wasn't possible for him to understand it all. But the bond had been strong enough that Tynan had listened to him and hadn't laughed at him. Maybe that should be enough.

"There something else on your mind?" asked Tynan, looking at his watch.

"No, sir. I just wanted to let you know that I believe in this ESP stuff. I have it. I can guess the cards that are being held up and I can sometimes see the future. Not always, and not always exactly right, but I can see it."

Tynan smiled. "Then you're in the right place. Maybe you should talk with Sumner-Gleason about this."

Davis dug in his pocket and pulled out several bills. He dropped them on the table and said, "Maybe I will."

"You need a ride?" asked Tynan, standing.

"No, sir. I'll walk on over to the motel. It's not that far and I can use the exercise." He ignored the fact that he had left his car at the naval base. He'd retrieve it the next day, or maybe he'd take a cab over to get it. He wouldn't let Tynan know that he'd left it there so that he could talk to him.

"Okay," said Tynan. "See you in the morning."

Tynan left the restaurant feeling strange. The conversation with Davis had bothered him more than he'd let on. After the discussion of ESP they'd had the day before, coupled with Davis's claims of precognition and the Navy's obvious endorsement of the topic, Tynan was worried. There was something more bothering Davis than he'd talked about, but Tynan had handled the situation poorly. He hadn't given Davis the opportunity to express himself. It was that damned question about Hitler. What could the relevance of that be? Was Davis suggesting that he had found a way of killing Hitler before he started the war?

Tynan sat in his car, the key in the ignition, but hadn't turned it on. He thought about what Davis had said and wondered exactly what the answer should be. He knew that killing wasn't the problem. He'd done that before in the line of duty. He'd sneaked up behind enemy guards and used a garrote to kill them, or a knife to cut their throats, or had shot them at close range with a pistol. It wasn't killing.

Maybe it was the magnitude of the death. Killing Hitler wasn't really the question. It was changing history that came into play. That was the hesitation. That was the reason that he didn't have a straight answer to the question. Take history out of the equation and he would have no remorse in killing the man. If anyone had ever deserved killing, it was Adolf Hitler. It was the result of that death on history that frightened Tynan. Without Hitler, things for the allies could have been much worse than they were.

Finally he started the engine and backed up. As he did, he saw Davis emerge from the restaurant. His face was pale and he looked as if he were going to pass out. Tynan pulled toward him and leaned across the seat to roll down the window on the passenger's side.

"Hey, you feeling okay?"

"Yes, sir. I'm fine."

"You want a ride?"

"No, sir, I want to walk. Thank you anyway."

Tynan shrugged and rolled up the window. He drove off, stopped long enough to look back and then pulled out into the traffic.

He drove back to the motel in a daze, thinking about everything Davis had said. Talk of Hitler and changing history and knowing the future. It was like he had been caught up in a science fiction novel where conventional science was lost to flights of fantasy. ESP and predicting the future were things that should be left to the science fiction writer and the tabloids that were found in grocery stores. It wasn't something that Navy personnel should be worrying about.

He pulled into the space in front of his motel room and parked the car. He went inside and headed to his room. As he dug his keys from his pocket, he thought about King and her background. Cultural anthropology. She would have looked into this sort of thing and would have some kind of an opinion. If nothing else, she would know where to look for more information about it.

He opened the door and all thoughts of ESP and Hitler and predicting the future deserted him. King was sitting on the bed, her back against the headboard. She turned toward him and smiled warmly. She wore no clothes; she was there, waiting for him without a stitch.

"Good afternoon," she said. "You're late." She grinned and added, "I'm cold."

Tynan kicked the door shut and moved toward her. He sat on the edge of the bed and reached to kiss her. "Sorry," he said.

"You stopped off with the boys for a beer. I'm here freezing to death and you're drinking beer." The smile didn't leave her face.

"Yes, but not much, and it was for a good cause."

"Well don't tell me about it now," she said. "I've other things on my mind."

"Right," said Tynan. And suddenly, so did he.

9

Davis returned to his motel room convinced that he was on his own. He couldn't ask his friends to help him, no matter what their background was. They wouldn't understand and he wasn't convinced that he would be able to tell them the truth. If he did, his next stop might by the psychiatric ward at the Great Lakes naval facility. He grinned at that and figured what the hell, it had a good view of Lake Michigan. Then, since he'd never been there, he wondered if it did. His ability seemed to leave him wondering on that point.

As he entered his room, he tossed his hat at the bed and then sat down staring at the thick phone book. The logical move was to look up Bainbridge's name in the book and give him a call. Talk to the man for a minute, thirty seconds, as he claimed that it was a wrong number and see what that did for him. See if it provided him with anything more.

He crossed to the bed, sat down on it and lifted the phone book from its nest under the nightstand. A heavy thing, three inches thick of just white pages. He flipped through it, looked for Bainbridge's number but couldn't find it.

"Of course," he said out loud. "The asshole's got an unlisted number."

He slapped it shut and then opened it again, letting his finger run down the column for Bainbridge. He hoped to pick up something, maybe a sister or brother or parents, but his mind remained blank. No clues about Bainbridge and his whereabouts now.

At random, he flipped open the book and again let his finger slip across the columns of names and numbers, unsure of why he was doing it. When he came to a listing for R. Sullivan, he stopped and looked at the number.

"R. Sullivan," he said and felt that it was important. And then he knew it was a woman's number. The single initial gave it away. Rachel was her name, he knew, even though that wasn't listed in the book. Rachel Sullivan had something to do with Jason Bainbridge. Davis didn't know what it was, but he knew there was a connection.

He leaned over and snagged the phone. Again he checked the number and then dialed it, not knowing what he was going to say to her if she answered. He waited while it rang, suddenly hoping that she wouldn't be home.

Finally she answered. "Hello."

"Rachel Sullivan, please."

"Speaking."

"Miss Sullivan, this is going to sound very strange, but I need your help to locate a Jason Bainbridge."

There was no response, but the phone seemed to grow cold in his hand. He felt that she was about to hang up and added hastily, "He's not a friend of mine. I don't think I'd like him, but I've got to find him."

For a few seconds more, there was no answer and finally she spoke. "Why?"

"Why indeed," said Davis. He had no answer for that. He had no answer for the dozens of questions that she could ask him. And then he knew what to say. He saw the dialogue as clearly as if it had been written down for him.

"Because he is a disgusting, evil man and there is something that needs to be done."

"Who are you?"

Davis decided to take a chance. "My name is Davis. I'm with the Navy."

Again there was silence, but she had stayed on the line. "Are you going to hurt him?" she asked, her voice quiet, the words almost lost in the buzz of static on the line.

Now it was Davis's turn to remain silent. Finally he said, "I'm going to get even with him. Or rather I'm going to try, but I'm going to need some help."

"What can I do?"

"Meet me for a drink somewhere." He thought about the pizza place where he'd talked to Tynan and suggested it.

"That's across town," she said. "How will I know you?"

"I'll know you. An hour enough time?"

"Yes."

Davis hung up then and leaned back. He drained his mind and tried to focus on Bainbridge but there was nothing there. He tried to conjure up the image that he'd seen earlier, of Bainbridge in the War Room, but nothing came. He could see the scene, as a memory of the earlier vision, but he could see nothing new about it. Everything was the same, faded slightly because it was now a memory. There wasn't the brightness, the richness of a vision as it came to him, and it seemed that he was living it. Just the dull images of an already partially forgotten memory.

He stood up finally and moved to the closet, where his civilian clothes hung. He grabbed a shirt and blue jeans and went into the bathroom to change.

Tynan was lying on his back, his hand under his head, staring up at the ceiling. King was next to him, also staring up. Both were covered with a light coating of sweat from their activity.

After five minutes, Tynan rolled to his side so that he could look at King. Finally he said, "Got a question I want to ask you."

"Go ahead."

"What can you tell me about ESP?"

She laughed and said, "I thought you were going to ask about something a little more romantic than that."

"Normally I would come up with something," said Tynan, "but tonight I want to ask you if you believe in ESP."

She sat up and then leaned over the edge of the bed, snagging the shirt that Tynan had worn. She slipped it around her shoulders and then slipped back so that she was against the headboard.

"The very term covers a multitude of talents, abilities and beliefs. To reject everything out of hand is not good science. There are aspects of it that I don't accept and others that I do."

"Like?"

"Well, I know the Russians are experimenting with astral projection . . ."

"What in the hell is that?"

She grinned at him and said, "Out-of-body experiences. There are some people who claim that they can project their souls, or their personalities, or their essence, out of their bodies and experience things far away. I think the Soviet plan is to train people to do that and then spy on their enemies. Send them out to learn state secrets."

Tynan had to laugh. The image of some Russian invading the Pentagon, a ghostly shape to spy on them, seemed funny. He shook his head and said, "You're kidding."

"Not at all. They really believe it, or maybe more accurately, they're really trying it. If it works, then it puts them one up on everyone."

"Could we see them?"

"That's the point where we get into a strange area. They might appear as a ghostly image and therefore give rise to stories of ghosts. It might just be mental energy that you couldn't see, but might be able to sense on some subliminal level."

Again Tynan laughed. "Well, I've always suspected that the Pentagon was haunted."

"The Soviets are also doing research on mind-reading techniques, telekinesis and the like. They're doing research into a dozen areas of the paranormal, and they're spending a lot of money on their reseach."

"Fine," said Tynan. "That doesn't mean it's anything real."

"Now," she said, her voice beginning to sound like that of a professor lecturing an undergraduate class, "there are things that we don't begin to understand. I've seen native rituals, ceremonies in Africa where the paranormal seems to work quite well."

Tynan got up, found his underwear and slipped it on. He moved to the combination luggage rack and TV stand, where the cans of Coke stood. He opened one, took a drink and then turned to face King.

"Wouldn't you say," he asked, "that the reason those rituals work is because the people believe they will work? It has nothing to do with the supernatural or paranormal but with the psychology of the situation?"

"Very good," said King. "There is something to be said for that explanation. Some of the trials by ordeal work because of the psychological beliefs of the people. But there are other things that can't be easily rationalized by modern science or conventional thought."

Tynan nodded and took a deep drink of the warm Coke. "Then your answer to my question is that you don't know. That no one really knows."

She shrugged. "I would think that such an answer would give you the information that you need. In other words, I don't reject anything out of hand. I know there are fakes and frauds, but that doesn't mean that everyone is a fake or a fraud; sometimes it seems that ESP, that the paranormal, influences the lives of the people who experience it."

"What about Jeane Dixon?"

King shrugged again. "There is good evidence that she did predict John Kennedy's assassination before hand. But in the predictions that have been widely reported since then, her score isn't all that great. Some of the others have been so far off the mark that it seems impossible that anyone would listen to her anymore."

"So we have nothing concrete, but the jury is still out."

King nodded and added, "Scientifically speaking, it is incumbent on those who claim a paranormal ability to prove that such an ability exists. Science should not be required to prove that it doesn't exist. When that begins to happen we have bad science and bad results."

"Meaning?" asked Tynan.

"Meaning," said King as she stood up, "that the current state of affairs is that the paranormal doesn't exist. Those who say they have talent should summit to scientifically structured tests, in the laboratories."

"So that scientists can claim that there is nothing to the abilities."

King moved closer to Tynan. The shirt she wore over her shoulders no longer covered her. There were flashes of her naked body beneath the material, and even with that, Tynan didn't want the discussion to end.

Kind said, "Most scientists have no ax to grind. They want to study the phenomena in the laboratory so that they can reproduce the results. If you claim that you can move an object with mental power alone and show that on a stage, then you should be able to do it in the lab. But everyone who has submitted to laboratory tests has been caught using trickery. Each of them has been proven a fraud when the cameras roll. That is why science is skeptical.''

''Well,'' said Tynan, slipping his hands around her waist, ''thanks for clearing that up.''

''Do you understand what I said?''

''Of course,'' said Tynan nodding. ''You said that science studies the phenomena but doesn't believe in it because they can't test the results in the lab. They can't reproduce the results in the lab.''

''It means that those who predict the future must give scientists the predictions before the events. None of this sealed envelope shit. It means that those who claim telekinetic power must be able to demonstrate the talent in the lab with the cameras running. It means that objective proof must be offered to science.''

''And that hasn't happened?''

''Not yet, though Rhine is getting some good results at Duke.'' She shrugged then and added, ''Although I understand that some of his results are being questioned now. Others haven't been able to reproduce his work so that his methodology is being questioned.''

Tynan suddenly decided that he didn't care about Rhine and his results at Duke. He didn't care about ESP and scientific research. He reached up and pushed the shirt from King's shoulders so that she stood there, in the half light given off by the bathroom fixture, completely naked.

''You hungry?'' he asked.

''Not for food.''

Bainbridge slowed the car once, looked over the woman standing at the corner of the building and decided that he didn't like her. The look was wrong. She was too hard, too experienced. There was nothing innocent left in her after years on the street. She'd make sure that he had his pleasure because that way she could earn a bonus, but that wasn't what he wanted. He wanted someone a little less hard.

He turned the corner and pulled to the curb. He sat there, watching as the people circulated on the street. There was a pool of light from a single lamp that illuminated the trees and bushes of the park, creating a back drop for the city. There were no colors visible, just blacks and whites, and the motion of the people as they moved across the background like extras in an old film.

Bainbridge leaned over and opened the glovebox. He took out a pack of cigarettes, shook one free and put it between his lips. He pushed in the lighter and then glanced up. She was coming across the sidewalk at him. A young, tall woman with long hair and knee-high boots. Her short skirt looked like a wide belt so that most of her thighs were bare. He liked the way they jiggled when she walked. She walked up to the car and tapped on the passenger's window. Bainbridge rolled it down.

She leaned in, giving him a clear view down her loose-fitting blouse. "You looking for a good time?"

Bainbridge looked up, into her face and into her eyes. There was a quality there, behind the bluster and the bravado. Not innocence, but vulnerability. That was it. She had a look of vulnerability.

"Sure," he said. "What's it going to cost me?"

"Hey," she said, "who said anything about money? I show you a good time, maybe you can show your appreciation a little later. That way everyone is happy."

"A hundred dollars is all that I have to spend."

She nodded once and then reached in to open the car door. As she slipped in, she managed to let her skirt hike up so that Bainbridge could see her lace panties. "I got a place close by," she said.

"You come to my place," he said.

"I don't know about that."

"I got only the hundred on me, but I have more at home. An extra fifty and you stay the night."

She grinned, showing pearly teeth. Someone had spent a great deal of money making sure that her teeth would be perfect when she grew up.

Bainbridge dropped the car into gear, glanced over his shoulder and pulled into traffic. As he did, the girl slid over so that her hip was against his. She reached down and let her fingers play across his thigh until they touched him and felt his response. She then looked up into his eyes, and smiled, showing her dimples.

"You're sure ready, honey."

Bainbridge reached for her hand and stopped the caresses. He held on to her and said, "We can wait for a moment. It's not that far."

He pulled into an underground parking garage, drove down several levels and then stopped, pulling into a space. He got out his side and waited for her. Together they walked across the darkened floor and out into a pool of light near the elevator. As he punched the button, he got a better look at her face. She couldn't be more than nineteen, if that. Her skin was smooth, unblemished, and her long dark hair seemed to shimmer with an eternal light. She had big blue eyes that gave her a look of innocence. She was absolutely perfect.

They rode the elevator in silence. Bainbridge studied his victim, thrilled with his selection. It had been so simple. She had come to him, asked him if he wanted a good time. The search was getting easier every time.

They walked down the hallway, brightly lighted and carpeted with a new shag. Bainbridge opened the door and pushed her in. She stumbled once and then caught her footing.

"Hey," she said as she turned to face him.

Bainbridge rubbed a hand on the wall until he found the light switch. When the lamps came on he pointed at her and demanded, "Strip."

"Sure, honey. Glad to." She grinned and began to slowly unbutton her blouse. She glanced up, smiled and then went back to work.

"Now. I want you naked."

She picked up the cue and hurried to get out of her clothes. She dropped them on the floor and then stood, facing him, completely naked. "There. You like?"

Bainbridge moved toward her, standing in front of her, only inches away. He gazed into her eyes, holding her attention that way. He doubled his fist and struck her, hard, in the stomach. For an instant there was a frozen look of pain on her face and then she fell to the floor, landing on her side. Her mouth worked like that of a fish out of water as she drew her knees up and wrapped her arms around her belly.

"Now," said Bainbridge. "We'll get down to business." He stood over her, waiting for her to regain her breath. Slowly she began to move, getting to her knees.

The girl then let out a startled cry. She tried to pull away from him, frightened by the look on his face, by the glow in his eyes. She knew that she had made a mistake now, and hoped that it wouldn't prove to be fatal. She prayed that he would just beat her up. That he wouldn't kill her.

Bainbridge grabbed at her, but she pulled away from him. He grinned evilly and said, "You're making it harder on yourself. You're making me angry and that will make it so much harder on you."

That made no difference to her now. She glanced at the door, measuring the distance and the angle and wondering if she could get by him and out. She feinted one way and went the other, but Bainbridge wasn't fooled. He grabbed her shoulder, spun her and struck again. A painful blow just below her right eye. The light faded slightly, becoming a dull glow. The images were suddenly in a soft focus. No longer was she exactly sure what was happening around her. She fell to the carpet and lay there for a moment, stunned.

Bainbridge moved in, picked her up and began hitting her repeatedly. The blows were hard, just enough to rattle her, to stagger her. She stood in front of him, wobbling back and forth, no longer feeling anything. Then he hit her a final time in the belly, twisting his fist as he struck. She fell to the floor unconscious.

For a moment he stood there looking down at her. A little blood on her face from a split lip. More from her nostrils, some of it splattered on her shoulders and her chest. She wimpered once but didn't regain consciousness. She didn't move at all after she fell.

"We have a full night of fun ahead of us," he told her, but she didn't move.

10

The moment Rachel Sullivan walked into the pizza parlor, Davis recognized her. Even if he hadn't been able to use his psychic ability, he'd have known her from the bruises on her face. Bainbridge hadn't hit her more than two or three times, but he had managed to blacken her eyes. There was a bruise on her cheek and swelling.

Davis moved across the floor and stepped to her just as the hostess reached her. Davis smiled at both women and said, "She's with me."

The hostess nodded and retreated. As she did, Sullivan asked, "Are you Davis?"

"Yes."

She looked at the floor. "I don't know why I came here. I'm not in the habit of meeting strange men in restaurants so far from my home. It's just not a survival trait for a young woman alone."

"I have a table," said Davis, ignoring her remark. He lead her to the corner where only a few hours before he'd talked to Tynan about shooting Hitler before he could start the Second World War. He watched as she slid in on her side of the booth and then sat down opposite her. There was a beer sitting there, in front of him.

"Would you like something to eat or drink?"

"Just a Coke."

"Uh-uh," said Davis. "I ordered a pizza. Mushrooms and onions."

"How'd you know that I love mushroom and onion pizzas?" she asked suspiciously.

Davis took a deep drink of his beer and then set the glass down carefully, staring at it. He wasn't sure what to tell her, what she'd believe. There was something black hidden deep in her mind and he thought that it was a hate of Bainbridge. A deep-seated fear of the man and a hate of him. He reached out and touched her hand and felt another psychic presence. She had a weak ability that she kept suppressed almost as if afraid of it. It had been the reason that she had hated Bainbridge from the moment she set eyes on him. She hadn't known why she had reacted so strongly to him, but she had.

Before he had to say anything, before he could say anything, the pizza arrived. The waitress set in it the center of the table and looked at Sullivan. "Can I get you something to drink with the pizza?"

"Just a Coke."

As the waitress disappeared, Davis said, "I need to learn something about Bainbridge. I need to learn everything about him. I need to know him."

"Why?"

Davis shrugged and said, "I have to." He knew that it sounded lame but hoped that her hate for the man would not cause her to probe further. Her hate should mask her good sense so that she would talk to him.

The waitress returned with the Coke, and then took off. Davis pulled a slice of pizza free, using his left hand to jerk the strings of cheese away, and took a big bite. Tears came to his eyes and he took a deep drink of his beer. "Hot!" he said unnecessarily.

She sipped her Coke and then got a slice of pizza. She

set it on the small plate in front of her to let it cool. "What do you want to know?"

"Where he works. What he does. Where he lives. Anything that you can tell me."

To gain some time to think, she used her fork to cut the pizza. She took a bit and chewed it slowly. "I'm not comfortable with this," she said finally.

Davis drained his glass and sat back. "I understand that. But this is information that I need to know."

"Why?"

Davis laughed. "A good question."

"I'd like an answer."

Davis knew that he'd reached the end of the rope already. She wasn't going to talk to him and was growing suspicious of him. He wished that he could see the immediate future now. That might give him a clue about how to proceed. It would also tell him if he would get the information, but his mind was blank. Nothing was coming at him and he wondered if she was automatically, subconsciously throwing up a screen that kept him from acting.

"I'm going to tell you a story that is going to seem impossible to believe. I'm going to tell you everything and all that I ask is that you keep an open mind until I finish. Then, if you don't want to help, you go ahead and leave. I'll still spring for the pizza and the Coke."

"I'm listening," she said.

So Davis took a chance and filled her in on everything, telling her about his success with guessing games and on the standard esper tests. He told her of his flashes of the future and how Bainbridge was going to gain the presidency near the turn of the century. He told her of the coming war, how Bainbridge would live for that because he would see it as a way of controlling the world. Bainbridge might see most of the world destroyed, but when it was over, he would believe that he would rule it all. More than any other man had ever ruled at one time and it made no difference to him that three quarters of it would be rubble and that seventy percent of the population would be dead. He would rule the whole thing.

All the time he talked, she listened. There was never any indication that she didn't believe him. Occasionally she stopped him to ask questions but then would fall silent, eating the pizza and listening to his story.

When he finally finished, she asked, "You really believe all this?"

"I do," he said.

"And why should I?"

"For one thing, it was the way that I found you. I was using the phone book, trying to find Bainbridge's address and when I failed, I was flipping through it and your name popped up at me almost as if it had been written in bright red letters. The rest of the page seemed to fade away. I knew that you would have something to tell me."

"Uh-huh," she said and then fell silent again.

There were things that Davis wanted to say. Ways that he could prove his case, but he knew that it was time to let her think. If she said no, he would have a chance to recover from it, and if she said yes, there was no reason to keep pressing. It would be time to begin to plan.

"What do you plan to do?" she asked.

"Let me ask you something first. If you had known, in 1930, what Adolph Hitler was going to do, would you have tried to kill him?"

It was a long evening for the girl. Bainbridge kept her on the edge of consciousness, using his fists and then cold water, waiting patiently for her. When it seemed that it was all over, that Bainbridge had done enough, had enough pleasure, he reached down to find something else. There was never a chance, after the first few minutes, for her to get away. She was never conscious enough to think of it.

Finally, Bainbridge was finished, drained, almost exhausted. He sat on the couch, leaning back, his head resting against the wall. He'd turned off the lights and had opened the curtain. Through the picture window he could see the lights of Chicago spread out in front of him, almost as if it were a black cape covered with jewels laid at his feet, sparkling lights of greens and reds and yellows. Through the sky a single light moved, giving the impression of some kind of glowing ship from outer space.

The girl, lying on her side, blood splattered on her body which was now covered with bruises, groaned once. She lifted a hand and let it fall back to the carpeting.

Bainbridge stood, glanced at her and moved through the living room into the kitchen. He opened the refrigerator and took out a bottle of champagne. Holding a towel over the top of the bottle, he opened it with a dull pop that sounded like a shot from a silenced weapon. He took down a glass, splashed some of the wine in it and then tasted it.

"Excellent," he said.

He filled the glass and then walked back into the living room. His clothes were scattered on the floor where he'd thrown them in the heat of his passion. He kicked them aside and then knelt next to the girl. She opened her puffed and swollen eyes but said nothing.

"I'm really very sorry for the pain that you've suffered, but it is something that you have brought upon yourself. Your selected occupation means that you are the plaything for anyone with the money to pay. You are a toy, and for those of us with the money and the power, you must play."

She didn't respond. She felt sick to her stomach. She felt like throwing up and was afraid to move, sure that motion would push her over the edge. If she didn't move, didn't think, then she might not get sick.

Bainbridge stood up and moved to the window. He

watched the dancing lights outside for a moment longer and thought about the things to come. Without turning, he said, "You will be well paid for your suffering tonight. Forget about the hundred dollars. I will give you a thousand. Of course, you will then have to forget about everything that happened here."

Bainbridge turned, but the girl still hadn't moved, and he wondered, briefly, if he had permanently injured her. Maybe there was a spinal injury and the girl couldn't move. That would mean he'd have to kill her, finish the job. There was no way he could buy his way out of the trouble that a permanent spinal injury would cause. He sat down on the couch and stared at her and wondered what it would be like to kill her. Was she conscious enough to feel pain? Was she conscious enough to know what was happening to her?

In his mind, he planned it all out. Strangulation seemed to be the way to do it. His hands around her neck, squeezing the life from her. He'd be able to look into her eyes and watch her reactions. Maybe he'd be able to witness the actual moment of death when the eyes glazed over.

Afterward there would be the problem of the body. By waiting until late, two or three in the morning, he could probably get her to his car without witnesses. Then he'd have to drive out of town, maybe fifty, sixty miles to get somewhere so that he could leave the body where it wouldn't be discovered for a couple of days, or with luck, weeks. Highly inconvenient but probably worth the effort.

The girl groaned again but still didn't move. Bainbridge lifted his glass to his lips and tasted the wine. He swirled the liquor and drank again, savoring the good life. Fine wines, fast, expensive cars, two luxury apartments and more money than he would ever need. And if, for any reason, he needed more, there were ways to get it. Easy ways. A couple of phone calls and there would be people falling all over themselves to give him all the money he needed.

Leaving the girl on the floor, he walked into his bedroom. He set the wine on his dresser and stepped into the bathroom. He turned on the shower, adjusted the spray and the temperature. When it was right, he got in and washed himself quickly. That done, he turned off the water and stepped out. He grabbed a towel and dried himself.

Back in the bedroom, he finished the wine and then selected his clothes. A work shirt, blue jeans and running shoes, but no socks. Dressed, he walked into the living room. The girl was lying on her back, staring up at the ceiling. Tears streaked her face as she cried quietly.

Spread-eagle like that, all her charms available and visible, Bainbridge felt his desire stir again. To the girl, he said, "So, you are wide awake now and maybe ready to go at it again?"

She didn't respond. She rolled to her side and drew her knees up, against her chest. Her slight body shook as she cried harder.

"It's really too bad," said Bainbridge. He didn't explain it to her, but he meant that he wasn't going to kill her. It was too much trouble to do it and it could cause more trouble than he was ready for. Instead he would pay her off and suggest that any report to the police would result in her death. And the police would probably do nothing about it because she was a prostitute anyway.

Bainbridge kicked her clothes at her and said, "Why don't you get dressed now." He sat down on the couch, an arm on the back of it, to watch.

For a few minutes it was quiet in the apartment. No sound other than the sobbing of the injured girl. She made no effort to get up or to get dressed. Bainbridge finally became impatient with her.

"Get dressed now!" he ordered her.

Slowly the girl moved, groaning as she straightened her legs. With a great deal of difficulty, she sat up and then didn't move for several seconds. Her breathing was rough, ragged, and her face glistened from the tears.

"I think you broke my ribs," she said. The words came out haltingly, spaced, as if it hurt to talk.

Bainbridge was on his feet then. He stood over her menacingly but said, "I will drop you at the hospital if you want. Extra money to pay the bills there. That satisfy you? That keep you quiet?"

She didn't answer. She reached for her blouse and slipped it on, moving with exaggerated slowness. Every motion, every breath sent ribbons of pain through her. She would gasp, groan, but she didn't speak.

Bainbridge made no move to help her. Instead he walked into the kitchen and poured himself another glass of wine. Then he watched as the girl got to her feet. For a moment she swayed, like a tree in a high wind, but she didn't fall. She finished dressing, but then couldn't get her boots on. The effort was just too much.

Finishing his wine, Bainbridge returned to the living room. He handed her a package containing over a thousand dollars in cash. The money meant nothing to him.

She accepted it without a word. She stood there for a moment and then took a step toward the door.

Bainbridge pushed passed her, opened the door and looked into the hallway. There was no one around, no one in the corridor. He didn't expect anyone to be there that late.

It seemed that she took forever to walk to the elevator as Bainbridge escorted her. Once inside, she sagged against the wall, but didn't ask Bainbridge for help, and he offered her none. When they reached the garage, Bainbridge hurried to the car, got in and drove back toward the girl. It wasn't that he was thinking of the long walk to it or how much pain she was in but that he could get her out of sight that much faster. He couldn't afford witnesses.

Without speaking, Bainbridge drove her back to the street where he had found her. He pulled to the curb, away from the street lights, and stopped. As she tried to open the door, he grabbed her shoulder.

"You understand that if you say anything to anyone about this, I'll find you. You have been well compensated for your time and any pain you suffered. But if you talk, there will be no one on Earth who can save you."

She didn't speak. She merely nodded, her eyes on the street. Safety was so close now. She wasn't going to die at the hands of this psychopathic madman. Now all she wanted to do was get out and find a way to get home. That was it. Get out before he decided that she should die.

Bainbridge let her go then. She pushed herself from the car and staggered across the sidewalk, to the wall of the building. As she reached it, Bainbridge pulled away, humming to himself. It had been more fun that he had expected it to be. The only problem was that the girl had survived. Maybe next time, with a little bit of prior planning, he could remedy that.

11

When Sumner-Gleason entered the classroom the next morning, he searched the faces of the assembled men and then asked, "Where is Mr. Davis?"

"He hasn't made it in yet," said Tynan.

Sumner-Gleason moved to the front and set his briefcase on the lectern. He leaned forward, hands clasped, elbows on his case and said, "He was the only one of you who showed any potential for this training. He was the only one who had any ability at all."

"What's that mean?" asked Jacobs. "He really could see the future?"

"I don't know about that," said Sumner-Gleason. "I just don't know about that. But he is the first person who I ever had score perfectly on the tests, and that makes me think there are other gifts he may have."

Tynan felt his stomach grow cold as he thought about the discussions the night before. Sweat popped out on his forehead and he knew that Davis was planning something strange as surely as he had ever known anything else. It was the only excuse for his absence. Davis had seen something in the future, had some vision that he believed demanded his action, and he had been searching for the answers the night before. That had been the reason for the strange behavior and the strange questions.

There was nothing that Tynan could have said that would have convinced others that he was right. It was intuition, or second sight, or an inspired guess that was based on the little information that he had, and he knew that it was right. It was his explanation of how ESP worked. There had been clues that the eyes and ears ignored but that the brain received. Putting the data together, he knew that Davis was out on some crusade that had nothing to do with the Navy or his mission in the Navy or this class.

Tynan stood up. "Maybe I better try to locate Davis and make sure that he is all right."

Sumner-Gleason nodded and said, "While you do that, Lieutenant, the rest of us can proceed with the instruction. We've yet to get into the dietary requirements and the practice exercises designed to enhance the esper capacity."

"I'll go with you, sir," said Jacobs.

Before Sumner-Gleason could respond, Tynan said, "Good." He looked at the other men and asked, "Anyone know where Davis was billeted?"

"Candlelight Motel. Room four-oh-two," said Starkey.

"Thanks." Tynan headed for the door with Jacobs right behind him.

"Lieutenant," said Sumner-Gleason, "the man has a unique talent. I've never seen anything like it. You'll need to handle him carefully."

"Yes, sir," said Tynan. "I'll keep that in mind." He left the classroom with Jacobs.

In the hallway, Jacobs said, "Just where are we going to search for him?"

"We're going to drive over and check out the motel. Five'll get you ten that Davis is shacked up with some woman and just didn't get to class yet."

"Stupid move," said Jacobs. "With a class as small as the one we have here, anyone who skips is going to be missed. And that man, Sumner-Gleason . . . what the hell kind of name is that anyway?"

Tynan laughed. "English, I think."

"Yeah, well, that Englishman seems to regard our partner in crime as the best student and that makes it very hard for him to miss a session."

"Whatever," said Tynan, shrugging. He walked down the hallway into the bright sunlight of the early morning. "At least this gets us out there for a couple of hours."

It turned out that Davis had spent the night with Rachel Sullivan. Neither of them had slept because they had been too busy making plans. Davis used a spiral-bound notebook to write down everything that he knew about the future world. He sat at the small oak desk, in a chair that wobbled under his weight, and wrote. Sullivan sat on the edge of the bed, a Coke in her hand, waiting patiently and watching him work. She wasn't interested in turning on the television or the radio.

Occasionally Davis looked over at her, but she was content to wait for him to complete his task. As he bent back to his work, he was surprised that she had so quickly accepted everything he had told her. She had believed that he could peer into the future and that he had seen a future where most of the Earth lay in blackened, disease-wracked ruins, a few of the lucky and powerful unaffected by the destruction. A few governmental officials who managed to insulate themselves from the suffering of the rest of the human race survived in relative splendor while the rest of the human race fought over the scraps. She had believed it all as he told her about it and had demanded the right to help prevent it.

Davis had shook his head at that and warned her, "We're comtemplating a murder."

"He deserves it" was all she said as she touched the side of her face carefully.

They had returned to his motel room and he had started to write down everything in his spiral notebook. Sullivan had asked him, "Why?"

"It helps me focus the thoughts. It'll help me vector in on Bainbridge."

She hadn't understood it but she had accepted it.

For over an hour, Davis wrote, turning the pages quickly, almost as if he was reading something written on them rather than putting down his own thoughts and visions. He had organized it logically, chronologically, starting with yesterday's date, when he'd first had his vision of the future where Bainbridge would rule, and putting down everything that he knew about that future. He included the names of the Presidents, how long they would serve, the ending of the Vietnam War, or rather of the American participation in it, then the new invasion by the North when the Americans refused to help. He put down the taking of Americans in Iran and Jimmy Carter's attempt to get them back. He wrote about the setbacks in the space program, the Russians in Afghanistan and the Iranians and Iraqis fighting a religious war that neither side could win. There were Marines in Lebanon and Americans in Grenada.

He listed it all carefully, putting in the dates and the circumstances, feeling as he did that he was a modern Nostradamus writing down a path for the world to follow in the future. He shook his head and realized he was chronicling a path it might follow. Unlike Nostradamus, he didn't disguise the predictions in verse but wrote in a prose style, and although he didn't understand all the words, he knew their value.

When he finished, he sat back, his hand aching. He looked at Rachel and saw her as an old woman, sitting in a wheelchair, staring at a Bible. She glanced up, almost as if looking at a calendar, and he knew that she would die fifty years in the future while the men with the power to save her life stood around arguing about the new hospital budget. He felt a powerful sadness in the vision and didn't know why. He didn't mention it to her.

She saw that he had finished and said, "Can I read it?"

He pushed the notebook at her and said, "Go ahead. You won't understand much of it. Hell, I don't, but it's all there. Everything that I've seen of the future. Everything that I could remember."

As she read through it her face turned pale and her breathing became rapid. In a hushed voice, she asked, "Are you sure about all this?"

"Of course. It's all true. Everything I've written down there will happen sometime in the future, unless I do something to stop it."

She closed the notebook and handed it back to him. "Can you stop it?"

"That's the one thing I don't know. I've never tried before. All the events that I've seen were things that were out of my reach, events that I couldn't influence. Either I was too young, too far away or simply powerless. Now I'm in the right place at the right time to do something about it."

"Is killing him the only way?"

Davis was nervous suddenly. The excitement coursed through him, making him want to get up and run. Instead he paced the room, from one end to the other, walking rapidly and gesturing broadly, almost as if he were suddenly crazy. He glanced at her and said, "People like Bainbridge have a way of overcoming every roadblock thrown in front of them. Because they are unscrupulous, they will stop at nothing: blackmail, threats, murder, bribery. Anything and everything to gain and hold power. Only death will stop him."

"Then that's what we'll have to do," she said. "We'll have to kill him."

Davis looked at his watch and discovered that it was nearly six in the morning. He wanted to get started as quickly as possible before she could change her mind. Or he could change his. "How do we find this Bainbridge now?" he asked.

"He'll be at work in a couple of hours. We can wait for him there and follow him."

"Or take him as he comes out of the building," said Davis. In his mind, he saw himself with a sniper rifle, shooting the man from five-hundred yards. One shot to drop the man and that would give him a five-hundred-yard headstart. That would get them both out of the area before the police could arrived seal up the scene of the crime.

"Why can't we just walk up to him and shoot him that way?" she asked.

"Let's do it my way," said Davis.

Sullivan looked at the floor and said, "But I wanted to help." She sounded like a child who had discovered that her mother had already baked the cookies.

"You'll have to help. You'll need to use binoculars to spot the target for me. I might be the one who pulls the trigger, but you're going to be the one who does the spotting so that I can pull the trigger."

She nodded. Davis again looked at his watch and decided that there was too much that had to be done. If he went to sleep now, it would be another day before they could act and another day might be too much. From what Sullivan said, it sounded as if Bainbridge was beginning to unravel, and if that happened, he might get out of reach. He might get out of the city and it could prove impossible to find him before it was too late.

Without a word to her, he went to the yellow pages of the phone book and searched for a gun store. He found an ad that claimed they opened early for the morning hunter and fisherman. Davis stabbed a finger at the phone book and said, "Can you find this place?"

"Sure."

"Then let's go." As he left the room, he picked up his notebook and then stopped. Something told him to leave it there. If everything worked out, he could retrieve it later. If it didn't, someone else might have a need for it. Someone else might be able to stop Bainbridge.

Bainbridge awoke with the sun pouring through the window into his bedroom. He rolled onto his back and opened his eyes, staring up at the ceiling. After the night's activities, he felt good, very good. There was something exhilarating about bending another person to your will, forcing a person to do everything that you wanted, no matter what her personal feelings were, and then keeping her from reporting the excesses to the authorities. There was a power there that seemed to reinforce, that seemed to revitalize him.

He threw the sheets off and stood up. He moved to the window and looked out on the city, already coming awake, the streets and freeways and tollways filling with people on their way to their mundane and trivial existences. If they had only known what it was like to live on the edge, to control others, to risk it all for a trifling of pleasure that was quickly gone. If they only knew how easy it was to gain power.

Bainbridge walked into the living room and saw a scrap of clothing that had belonged to the girl. Her black lace panties, ripped now, lay kicked under the coffee table. For an instant, he thought of keeping them, like a trophy of success, but realized that would be foolhardy. It was one thing to risk it all to control the mind and body of another and something else to risk it for a scrap of cloth. If he felt the need for such a trophy, he could always get another. He would dispose of them on his way to work.

As he fixed himself breakfast, he turned on the television to get the latest news. From Vietnam it wasn't all that bad. Enemy forces had been pushed out of their stronghold at great loss of life for them. American casualties were described as light.

"Of course," said Bainbridge. "They always are."

He drank his juice while the TV journalists listed crimes of passion, murders, rapes, beatings and robberies. They talked about the budget and the space program and unrest in the Middle East but they didn't mention the vicious attack on a Chicago prostitute.

"Keep at it," he told them. "Just keep at it."

When he finished breakfast, he left the dirty dishes on the table because the maid, who came in for two hours every day, would take care of them for him. He walked into his bedroom and then into the bathroom. He got ready for work, taking his time because Smith would never have the guts to fire him. Not after he had found Smith and his young secretary locked in an embrace, the girl's skirt hiked up to her waist and Smith's hands in her panties.

He laughed at the image and then of Rachel trying to convince Smith to fire him. He'd told her that she handled it wrong. She just didn't know how wrong.

He dressed and left for the office. On the way, while stopped at a red light, he opened the door and dropped the prostitute's panties into the street, tossing them back, under his car. He'd seen other drivers do the same a hundred times. Get rid of the morning trash at the light.

Within a few minutes, he had parked his car and was at his desk, shoving papers around. He couldn't concentrate on the documents, his mind alive with the images of the night before. It had been a very good night.

*　　*　　*

The building was a long, low affair made of sheet metal
and painted a dull blue. There was a huge sign that adver-
tised guns, ammo and sporting goods. There were signs in
the windows telling customers that the prices were the
lowest in the Chicago area, and that if it couldn't be found
inside, it couldn't be found anywhere in the Free World.

Davis parked the car and walked across the lot. Sullivan
was right behind him, unsure of what she was supposed to
do. Davis opened the door for her and then followed her
in. The interior looked almost like a warehouse. Rows and
rows and stacks and stacks of sporting goods. Everything
from the camouflage clothes that the weekend sportsman
had to have, to the rods and reels that would land a shark,
if there had been any in Lake Michigan to catch. There
were sections for the golfer, the tennis player and the
baseball fan. There were bats and gloves and uniforms.
There were rubber boats and canvas tents. There were
outdoor stoves and Coleman lanterns. There were knives
and machetes and hatchets and axes. And along one wall
at the rear were hundreds of rifles and shotguns. Without a
word to Sullivan, Davis drifted in that direction.

There were two clerks on duty, but both of them ignored
Davis as he looked at the rifles. There were small caliber
and large. Lever action and bolt action. There was an
AR-15, the civilian, semi-automatic version of the M-16.
There were mini 14s and there were elephant guns. There
were rifles with fixed sights and adjustable. There were
scoped weapons in a variety of calibers. Davis leaned over
the glass counter that held a few pistols, more than a few
knives and some fishing reels. He studied the weapons
until he spotted the Model 70 Winchester that was like the
weapons used by the Marine snipers in Vietnam. It was
exactly what he wanted.

As the clerk came forward, Davis asked to see the rifle.
The man stopped, grabbed a set of keys from a drawer and
then unlocked the rack where the rifle was displayed.

When he handed it over the counter to Davis, he said, "You couldn't have picked a better rifle. The Marines are using them to kill the Viet Cong at a thousand yards or better in South Vietnam."

Davis took it and worked the bolt. It operated smoothly. He checked the breech and then looked into the barrel, making sure that it wasn't pitted by rust. He flipped it around and sighted through the scope.

"Finest weapon made," said the clerk.

"A nice weapon," agreed Davis. "What about range facilities to zero it."

The clerk nodded and smiled. "Ah, a man who knows his business. Well, naturally the scope and the weapon have been zeroed and test-fired before it was put out on display by our expert."

"But everyone is different. Someone else cannot zero a weapon for me."

"Of course. We have a range behind the store where you can zero the weapon if you so desire, but it's really unnecessary. You'll find that we've taken care of that problem. It's not like you're going to be shooting at something a thousand yards away with your life on the line."

"Still, I'd prefer to do it myself."

"Of course."

"What about the gun-control laws?" asked Sullivan.

"Well, the Feds won't let us sell rifles, or any guns through the mail, and there are some forms for the pistols, but for a sporting rifle, there really isn't that much trouble. You can't rob a store with a high-powered rifle." The clerk laughed and added, "Well, I suppose you could, but that hasn't happened around here for a long time."

"I'd like to test-fire this before I make a commitment on it," said Davis.

"Of course, sir."

"And the lady would like to find a good pair of binoculars here."

"Tom," said the clerk, "can you help the lady while I take this man out to the range?"

"Surely."

Davis nodded to Sullivan and then followed the clerk out to the range. As they moved to set up the targets, Davis realized that buying the weapon and getting into position to take out Bainbridge were going to be the easiest of the tasks. Getting away cleanly afterward was going to be the real trick. But then, given the stakes, he wasn't sure that getting away was all that important.

And then he remembered the vision of his death in Vietnam. Maybe getting away wasn't an option afterall. Maybe he should get caught so that he could save his own life. Prison might not be that pleasant, but it was sure a hell of a lot better than dying in the jungle.

With his mind, he reached out, trying to see into his future, or that of Bainbridge, but everything was blank. He shook himself and followed the clerk out to the range. He'd worry about the consequences later.

12

Tynan stood in front of the door and knocked again. Then he put his ear against the wood and listened, but there was nothing but silence on the other side of it. He glanced back at Jacobs and said, "He's either a heavy sleeper or he's not in there."

"We could go to the lobby and use the house phone."

"Which would do us no good if he's not in there." Tynan rubbed a hand through his hair. "I'm not sure what the next move would be."

"We could tell the manager that we need to get into the room."

"Why?" asked Tynan. "Because Davis was being a bad boy and didn't come to school?"

"Just a thought."

"Okay," said Tynan. "Let's try the house phone, and if that doesn't work, then let's write a note and slip it under the door. Tell him to call when he gets the chance."

"Old Sumner-Gleason isn't going to like it."

"Tough shit," said Tynan. He turned and walked down the hall, passed the fire extinguishers, a candy machine that had empty over most of the little windows, a Coke machine, an ice machine and a bank of pay phones. There wasn't a house phone among them.

They entered the lobby where they spotted another bunch of phones including a small white house phone. Tynan stepped to it, tried to raise Davis and then hung up. He shook his head when Jacobs looked over at him.

"Now what?"

Tynan looked at his watch and saw that it was only the middle of the morning. "I don't want to drive back to the base and listen to Sumner-Gleason talk about ESP right now. I think I'll move the search over to my motel room and see if Davis has shown up there."

"And what am I supposed to do right now?" asked Jacobs.

"Drop me off there and come back to collect me about one. We looked for Davis, waited for him to call, but that never happened. It's not our fault."

"Fine," said Jacobs.

Tynan went to the desk, got a sheet of paper and scribbled a quick note to Davis, telling him to call Tynan at the motel before one or to get to the class that afternoon so that Sumner-Gleason wouldn't call the Navy to cause trouble. As they left the motel, they slipped it under his door.

As Tynan stood up, Jacobs said, "Maybe we should break in and take a look around."

Tynan shook his head. "No reason for that. We don't know that anything is wrong in there. Maids will be going in soon anyway. We'll just wait."

They went out into the parking lot, got into the car with Jacobs behind the wheel. They drove over to the motel and Tynan got out. He went inside, knocked on the door to warn King that he was coming in and then entered.

"What are you doing here?" she asked. She was still in bed, watching television.

"I managed to escape for a while and didn't want to go back right away. Thought that we could find something to do if we put our minds to it."

She tossed the sheet aside and said, "I'm sure we can."

It had turned out to be exceedingly easy to buy the rifle. The dealer hadn't even asked to see any identification. Davis made it clear that he had never been convicted of a crime and was a good, upstanding citizen. He had paid for the weapon with a credit card which had eased any fears that the dealer might have had. The little plastic rectangle seemed to indicate that Davis was a man of honor.

Along with the rifle, he bought the binoculars, extra ammo and a case that looked more like it held fishing gear than a high-powered rifle. Once that was all accomplished, they went back out to Rachel's car; this time she drove.

As they pulled out of the parking lot, she asked, "Where exactly, or what exactly are we going to do now?"

"Let's drive on down to Bainbridge's office so that I can get a look at the lay of the land. If there is nothing there, then we'll need to get into position to follow him."

"Why not do that anyway?"

"We'll see," said Davis. "Right now our options are wide open and I want to keep them that way. This is too important for us to screw up because we got ourselves set on one course of action."

They rode in silence for a while. Davis leaned his head against the back of the seat and closed his eyes. With his mind, he reached out and tried to make contact with Bainbridge, or with the images that he had seen earlier, but that didn't happen. Too often, when he tried to force things, his mind remained blank. He had to let it come to him naturally. That was why he had such a wide range of impressions. Those events that had psychic energy were easy for him to see. Events that affected the course of the human race, or a large portion of the population, were the easiest. When he tried to narrow it, the various streams and eddies of the psychic world became confused, like someone was trying to project two or three movies on the same screen. Splashes of color and bits of sound overrode the rest of the images, and it was hard, sometimes impossible to pull out a single impression.

At the moment, there was nothing. Just the random thoughts that flowed through everyone's mind. Impressions from his past, thoughts about the future, and a sudden desire for Rachel Sullivan. He opened his eyes and looked at her. A good-looking woman, if you ignored the bruises and the blackened eyes, flaws that would heal. Then he shoved the feelings to the side, out of his mind, and again tried to touch Bainbridge.

This time he was hit with a wall of evil. If he had believed in demons, he would have thought that he had touched the mind of such a creature. There was a well of evil that seemed to bubble to the surface and then it was gone. Davis knew he had felt the mind of Bainbridge, had touched it briefly, and that frightened him.

He opened his eyes and sat up. Trying to bury the thoughts, the feelings for a moment, he asked, "Are we close?"

"Very," said Sullivan.

Davis nodded and looked around. Tall buildings, fifteen, twenty stories high. Not like the huge skyscrapers downtown, but tall enough. There was a park to one side, tall trees surrounded by gardens. Women and children and a few men were walking or sitting or playing.

"Pull over," said Davis.

Sullivan didn't respond. She did as she was told, and as soon as the car had stopped, Davis was out. He stood on the sidewalk, looking at one building and then up at another. When Sullivan joined him, he pointed and said, "Bainbridge works in there. Uses that door and leaves his car in the lot right there."

"Yes."

"Okay," said Davis. He took a step back so that his feet were on the grass and looked up at the rooftop of the buildings opposite of where Bainbridge worked. There was one that was higher than the others. There seemed to be a parapet, complete with a protective wall around it, that dominated the whole area. From there, he could control the rooftops as well as the streets around it. He wasn't sure why he felt that was necessary, but knew that it was.

"Right here," he said.

"What?"

"It has to be here," said Davis. "It seems right. It is right."

"What'll I do?" asked Sullivan.

"First thing, we've got to take the high ground. Then you'll have to act as the spotter. You'll have to watch for him. Once he comes out the door, you let me know and then I'll take the shot as quickly as I can."

"We go now?"

Davis smiled. "No, I don't want to go stumbling around with the rifle in my hands. We'll find a path up to the hide and then come back for the equipment."

"Hide?" asked Sullivan.

"The place from where I'll shoot. Called the blind by duck hunters."

"Oh."

After Sullivan locked the car, they crossed the street. They walked along the sidewalk as Davis looked into the windows of the stores there. They came to an office building and entered it. There was a directory on the wall near a bank of elevators, and although there was no guard on duty, there was a desk for one. It seemed that he came on after four and left about midnight, replaced by one who stayed until eight.

They took the elevator to the top floor and then found a stairway that lead to the roof. Davis ignored the signs that warned unauthorized people to stay away. He opened the door and stepped out into the morning sun.

The tower with the parapet was off to the right. He walked over there and found an old, rusting fire-escape ladder that led to it. Davis walked to the edge of the roof and looked down on the street. It provided a perfect view of the door where Bainbridge would appear, and of the parking lot where his car had to wait.

"It's perfect," said Davis.

Sullivan looked down and then at Davis. Sweat covered her face and stained her clothes. Her skin was pale and she looked like she was going to be sick.

"You okay?"

"I'm fine," she said.

"Sure. Listen, you can describe him for me and then get out. Hell, you really don't have to do that. I know what he looks like. I can take it from here alone. You've done everything that you can."

"No," she said, her voice taking on new strength. "I'm in this with you. Now, what do you want to do?"

"Let's go back down, get some food and then come back up here. I'll want something to drink because it's probably going to be hot up here by midafternoon. Once we've got that, we come back here to wait."

They left the roof and rode back to the street. They walked along until they found a sandwich shop and bought the food they were going to need. The only problem was the beverage, but it turned out they could buy a six-pack of Coke, and although they wouldn't be able to keep it cold, they would at least have something to drink.

They returned to the car and got the rest of the equipment. While the kids played in the park and their mothers yelled at them, Davis got the rifle out of the trunk. He leaned it against the rear bumber and then looked at the people around him. They were paying no attention to him.

If he remained calm, moved with determination, like a man hurrying to work, but didn't run, no one would look at him.

He picked up the rifle, disguised in its case, and waited as Sullivan got the binoculars from the backseat. Then they walked across the street, along the sidewalk and ducked into the office building.

Again, no one stopped them as they went to the roof. They saw no one in the hallways although they heard them behind the closed doors. On the roof, Davis stopped long enough to jam the door shut, making it harder for anyone to follow them up. Then he moved to the ladder. He jumped, pulled it down and then scrambled up it. He climbed over the wall and dropped onto the parapet, finding that it was three-feet wide. There was a single access door and Davis knew that he could jam it shut too, so no one would be able to sneak out of it and surprise him.

He returned to the ladder and climbed down for more of the equipment and food, which he carried up with Sullivan right behind him.

Once everything was there, he arranged it so that he could get at it. He took the rifle from the case and pulled the caps from the scope. Standing back, away from the wall so that no one below would see the barrel of the weapon, he looked down into the parking lot. By taking a single step forward, he would be able to see the whole thing. He could also see the door that Bainbridge would probably use.

He knelt and set the rifle on the open case, making sure he didn't jar the scope. Staying on his knees, he looked over the top of the wall and down into the street.

"Now, one of us will have to keep watch all the time. We don't want him sneaking out while we're not looking. It'll be best if we both watch, but not necessary. Besides, each of us will need time to rest."

"You sound like you've done this sort of thing before," said Sullivan.

Davis snorted once and then shrugged. "I've had the opportunity to use a long range rifle before on one or two missions." He pulled the pop-top on one of the Cokes and drank deeply.

Sullivan moved around so that she could see the doorway and then settled in to watch. There were a hundred questions she wanted to ask, but didn't. Instead she thought about what they were about to do and wondered how she had allowed herself to be talked into it. Was it because the man had hit her and then cost her her job? Certainly not a capital crime. Was it because she hated him that she allowed Davis to drag her into this conspiracy to murder another man?

She kept the binoculars on the doorway, watching the comings and goings of the people. She looked into the faces of them and wondered if she shouldn't just get out now. Davis had said that he could do it, but she didn't feel right about that. If she felt strongly about Bainbridge, she would have called it off and gotten out. But now it was too late. The die was cast and she was involved even if she got out now.

She glanced at Davis, who was leaning on the top of the wall, his hands cupped over his eyes, shading them. He glanced at his watch and asked, "Does he go out for lunch?"

"I don't know."

"Let's be alert," said Davis, "it's close to lunchtime." He crouched then, picked up his rifle, worked the bolt and loaded it. He popped the caps from the telescopic sight and stepped back. For a moment he used the sight, putting the crosshairs on the door, watching as a woman exited.

As Davis crouched down, Sullivan saw Bainbridge in the doorway. For a split second she was silent and then said, "There. That's him."

Davis leaned, grabbed his rifle and stepped to the wall. As he raised the weapon to his shoulder and swung it around so that he was looking down into the street, he dropped to his right knee and used the top of the wall for a bench rest. The crosshairs centered on Bainbridge. As he looked through the scope, he again felt the evil that was coursing through the man. The psychic energy surrounding him was almost a visible, pulsating evil cloud.

Davis didn't fire as Bainbridge turned into the parking lot. He knew that his target would be standing still as he tried to unlock the car. Through the limited field of vision, he could see no other people, just Bainbridge, a small man with greased-down hair, wearing a light gray suit.

The man stopped at the door of his car, and as he fumbled his keys from his pocket, Davis took a deep breath, exhaled, took another and began to squeeze the trigger. He kept his eye on Bainbridge, and just as the weapon fired, Bainbridge ducked. The bullet smashed into the car behind Bainbridge, shattering the window.

"I don't believe it," said Davis. "I don't fucking believe it." He worked the bolt, extracting the cartridge.

"What? How?"

"Shut up," snapped Davis. He swung around but couldn't see Bainbridge. Davis couldn't believe the man would be smart enough to roll under a car. Almost everyone was trying to see what was going on, but he took cover.

"Do you see him? Do you see him?"

Sullivan was confused, frustrated. She raised the binoculars to her eyes and scanned the parking lot. There were people running, dodging and hiding. Although only one shot had been fired, everyone seemed to have figured out what happened and were running for cover. All were still visible as they scrambled around. All except Bainbridge. He seemed to have vanished as completely as Judge Crater.

"Do you see him?" demanded Davis.

"No. No!"

"I don't believe it."

"What happened?" asked Sullivan. She shot a glance at Davis and then turned back to the binoculars.

"He dropped the keys and bent over."

Sirens began to wail in the distance. Far off sirens that meant the police were on the way. Davis didn't take his eyes off the parking lot and the car where he thought that Bainbridge was hidden. He couldn't believe that the man stayed where he was, his head down. It showed that the man was smarter than the average civilian. It showed that Bainbridge knew better than to stick his head up.

"Get up. Get up," said Davis.

"Now what?" asked Sullivan.

"Keep watching," ordered Davis. He wanted to tell her to shut the fuck up and do her job, but remembered she was a civilian. She knew nothing about lying in wait for the enemy. She was frightened and inexperienced and talking too much, too fast. She was nervous.

Below, the sirens had gotten closer. There was a squeal of tires and Davis knew the police had arrived. It would be two, three minutes before they knew what was happening here. There would be conflicting stories from the civilians, but the police would soon be able to figure it out. The two or three minutes that they would waste trying to learn the situation might be all that he needed.

It might be, but Davis didn't think so. He'd already blown it.

13

The instant the window shattered, Bainbridge knew what had happened. He had been prepared for something like it for years. An angry whore, a blackmail victim, a friend of one of the victims. Someone out to get even with him. Someone with gun who wanted him dead.

Bainbridge crawled under the car, on his belly, sliding away from the gas tank to use the front tires as a shield. He looked out toward the street but could see no one there. He waited for a second shot, but there wasn't one. The gunman, whoever he was, was a pro. Knew what he was doing. But time would be working against him now.

Bainbridge couldn't see much, just a few feet of the people who were running for safety. No one was diving under the cars. They were scrambling for doors and the rear of the parking lot, trying to get out of the line of fire. Plenty of targets for the rifleman, if he was interested in shooting people at random. If he was like the man in the tower in Texas, the victim would make no difference. The fact that he wasn't shooting meant he'd had one target and Bainbridge knew who it was.

Suddenly, Bainbridge was afraid. The killer was waiting for him. The logic of it was inescapable. He felt sweat bead on his body and begin to drip. His clothes were clammy, uncomfortable. There was a knot in his stomach, a cold lump there as he began to believe he was about to die. He was aware of the rough concrete and the odor of dirt and oil and gas.

And then came the distant wail of a police siren. Bainbridge closed his eyes tightly, almost as if that could hold off the killer until the police arrived. His lips moved in silent prayer. He promised much, if he could just live through the next few minutes.

The siren was getting louder and then was joined by another and another. Police from all over were racing to the scene of the shooting. Bainbridge pushed himself to the rear, under the engine of the car, until his feet hit the wall around the lot. He stayed where he was, the breath rasping in his throat and the sweat soaking his clothes.

A police car turned onto the street and screeched to a halt. The siren died, but the emergency lights continued to flash. One door opened and a police officer tumbled out, using the car for a shield. He crouched there, behind the door, his eyes roaming the street and then the buildings, not sure of the trouble or the danger.

From somewhere a man's voice shouted, "He's on the roof across the street. Behind that wall. Got a rifle."

The cop tossed his hat into the car and duckwalked toward the rear of the vehicle. He poked his head up and searched the rooftops for the gunman.

His partner crawled across the seat and dropped out the same door. He stepped around it and then turned, facing the building where Bainbridge worked.

"You see what happened?" the cop asked of the hidden voice.

"Guy up there took a shot at the people in the parking lot. Everyone scattered and he hasn't fired again."

The cop turned and looked up.

Bainbridge, feeling braver now, slipped forward and

tried to peek out from under the car, but he could see nothing. Instead, he moved to his right and slid clear but stayed on the ground. If the man was on the rooftops, he wouldn't be able to see him. Bainbridge was safe, just as long as he didn't stand up. He'd have to stay where he was until the police either captured or killed the gunman.

Two more police cars arrived. They blocked off the street. One of the officers ran down the sidewalk opposite them, so that the gunman above couldn't see him. As long as he stayed next to the fronts of the buildings, the angle would be all wrong and the gunman wouldn't be able to see them.

Other cops began arriving, some of them stopping on the side streets. They were infiltrating the area slowly, moving from car to car to building and back again, filling in the gaps, surrounding the area so that the gunman couldn't get away. They wanted to make sure they got him.

From the parapet, Davis could see everything that was going on below him. The first cops who had arrived had shown themselves a dozen times, and if Davis had wanted to kill them, he could have. Now those running through the streets were making targets of themselves. He could have dropped a dozen of them. That would have slowed them down as they tried to figure out how to storm the tower. But then, Davis had no quarrel with them. He was interested only in Bainbridge.

He stood there, back from the wall so that he could see down into the parking lot, his eyes on the car where Bainbridge hid. The man was still there; he knew it. There had been no chance for him to get away.

He raised a hand and wiped the sweat from his face. Suddenly it seemed hotter on the parapet. It wasn't the sun, but the situation. He glanced to where Sullivan crouched, her head bowed as if searching for something she'd dropped near her feet. She hadn't moved since he fired the shot.

Police officers, some of them wearing helmets, were running from car to car. They were using the available cover to move closer. To Davis's trained eye, they were a bunch of amateurs. They didn't know how to use the cover they had. They exposed themselves for too long and made their destinations too obvious. They had dealt with amateurs for so long that they didn't know how to do it themselves, if they ever had. He could have dropped them as they moved if he'd wanted to.

He shook himself, trying to concentrate on the task at hand, but something else kept intruding. The shot, no more than five-hundred, six-hundred yards, had been a simple one. A man used to a scope, looking down at the target, shouldn't have missed a stationary man. Fate had intervened. Fate had stopped him from killing Bainbridge.

In that instant, Davis wondered if the future could be changed. God, or the spirits, or the universe, or something had decreed that Bainbridge would launch a nuclear war, and it looked as if having the knowledge and the opportunity to do something about it weren't enough to change it. Bainbridge still lived and Davis's chances of changing it were slipping away.

From the street a voice, amplified electronically, shouted, "You, in the tower. We've got you spotted now. We've got the place surrounded. There is no way out."

"Right," said Davis, knowing that he could shoot his way clear if he wanted to. The police didn't expect that sort of thing. They expected him to stay in the tower, taking potshots at people as they moved around. They weren't ready for someone who knew how to handle the high-powered weapon, who knew how to kill, and who knew how to escape and evade whether the terrain was jungle or urban.

"What'll we do now?" asked Sullivan. Her voice was high, tight. She was badly scared.

Davis wasn't scared. He was pissed. He'd missed a simple shot and it didn't look as if he was going to get a second one. Bainbridge was too smart, or too cowardly, to show himself while the rifleman was still out there. He'd stay put until the danger had passed.

He shook his head, telling himself there was no reason to stay now. Bainbridge was warned and safe. He wouldn't be able to get him. The streets were filling with cops, many of them armed only with revolvers and shotguns, but there were a few rifles in the bunch. He had failed.

"If you do not give up, we will be forced to open fire," boomed the voice.

"Dennis, what'll we do?"

As she spoke, the police opened fire, a rippling of pistol shots and the booms of shotguns. Davis ducked instinctively. He heard bullets snap overhead, heard them strike the concrete of the wall behind him. Some of them whined off into the sky. There were pops and snaps as the rounds smashed into the solid wall. Chips of rock bounced around the deck.

"Oh, God," said Sullivan, her voice high and squeeky. "Oh, God."

"Relax," said Davis. "They can't hit us."

"What'll we do?" she demanded.

Davis laughed then. The whole situation was stupid. He hadn't planned on an alternative escape route because he expected to be on the ground before the police could arrive. He had figured to drop Bainbridge and then get out. Now that wouldn't happen, not burdened with Sullivan. She would slow him down. She would cause him to be caught. It had been stupid to bring her after she had bird-dogged Bainbridge for him.

"Well," he said, "I sure fucked this one up."

"What'll we do?"

"I've got to get out." He stopped talking as the firing from below tapered. He knew the police would be trying to get up at him now. He had to slow them for a moment.

Without a word to Sullivan, he popped up, put a round through the front tire of the patrol car on the street below him. He worked the bolt, swung the weapon and put a bullet into the emergency light bar, shattering it.

As the return fire started, he dropped down, lying flat. He listened to the shooting. It was uncoordinated. There was a volley of six rounds from each of the police revolvers, and then a tapering as the men reloaded. There were quick booms from a number of shotguns and then silence. A few moments later, as the men had reloaded, the firing picked up again.

Davis laughed out loud.

"What the hell is so funny?"

"Those guys down there aren't coordinating their fire. In Vietnam we'd attack when almost all of them were out of ammo and reloading."

"What in hell are you talking about?"

Davis turned and looked at her, a beautiful woman who was badly frightened. Her pale face was bathed in sweat. Her eyes were wide open, the pupils gigantic.

"Never mind," said Davis quietly. "Just never mind."

"Are we going to get out of here?" she asked, sounding like a frightened little girl.

"I don't know yet," said Davis. He shook his head and then added, "Looks like we can't change the future."

"One hell of a time to find out," she said.

Davis stared at her and said, "We had to try. With Bainbridge, we had to try."

"What are we going to do now?"

Davis was about to tell her that he had no idea what they were going to do, and then suddenly he did. He didn't know if it would work or not, but it was better than sitting there, waiting for the police to shoot them to pieces.

Tynan sat at the tiny table, eating the room service sandwich he had ordered. King sat opposite him, eating a salad of wilted lettuce and pink tomatoes. In the background, they had the TV on, waiting for the news at noon, but neither was paying attention to the game show in progress.

Tynan was wondering how much longer he should let the class go on. It had been three days and they really hadn't done much except spend a great deal of the taxpayers' money. Even after the things that King had told him, he wasn't sure it was worth it. Not when there were radios and hand signals that could do the job without a great deal of specialized training. He'd have to say something to the commandant soon.

King asked, "Do you have to go back this afternoon?"

"I suppose I'd better. There are three of us missing right now so that really cuts into the class size." He took a drink of his Coke and then said, "I really had expected Davis to check in by now. If there was one of us who seemed suited for this from the beginning, it was him."

King shrugged and continued to eat. Tynan looked past her at the television and then turned his attention to his own food. He picked up the sandwich and then saw the *Special Bulletin* sign flash.

He leaned forward and heard the announcer sounding breathless. ". . . gunman fired one shot before police arrived. Shots between the gunman and the police have been exchanged, but so far no injuries have been reported . . ."

On the screen the camera was panning to show the

police officers crouched by their vehicles, their weapons drawn. All of them were looking up, at a building across the street. The camera pulled back, showing a dozen policemen against the wall on the other side of the street. They weren't moving, just standing there, wearing bullet-proof vests, dark baseball caps and carrying M-16s.

The angle of the shot changed as the camera was tilted so that it showed the parapet where the gunman was hidden. There was nothing to be seen there. If the gunman was up there, he was staying out of sight.

King turned in her chair and glanced at the TV. "What is it?"

"Gunman downtown taking potshots at people." Tynan thought about the man in the tower in Texas. He'd dropped twenty-five or thirty people before the police got to him. Random shooting, just firing at anyone who moved or who came into his range of fire, killing innocent people.

On the television the reporter was already drawing the parallels, but then claimed that local police had contained the man so quickly that no one had been hurt. There had been some property damage, but no casualties.

"Doesn't make sense," said Tynan.

The phone rang then. Tynan pushed back his chair and leaned across the bed to get it. "Hello."

"This is Harison. You got the TV on?"

"Yeah, Harison. Why aren't you in class?"

"Nevermind that. You see the story about the gunman downtown? Well, I think that it's Davis."

"What in hell are you talking about?" demanded Tynan, although he already knew. As soon as the words had been spoken, he knew that they were right. It explained the talk about killing Hitler before he could destroy Europe and kill millions of people in a war.

"Dennis thought that he was on some kind of mission.

Talked about it to me, just briefly, but I know that's him down there. I just know it," said Harison.

"He give you any clues about the mission? He tell you why he thought he had to do it?"

"No sir, but I know that's him."

Tynan shot a glance at King and then looked at his watch. "Where are you?"

"At the motel."

"Okay," said Tynan. "I want you to pick me up here as fast as you can. Then we'll get down there and see if we can't talk to Davis, if it is him. Get him down from there before someone gets killed."

"Maybe I should go by his room," said Harison.

"What in hell for? There's nothing in the room that's going to help us now."

"Yes, sir. I'll be there in ten minutes."

King was on her feet then. She had moved closer to the television and turned up the sound. The reporter was still jabbering about no one knowing what was happening or who the gunman might be or what his motive was for shooting at people.

"I'm going with you," she said.

"Why?"

"Because."

"Not much of a reason," said Tynan. He put on a khaki uniform shirt with his rank on the collar. If the gunman was Davis, he wanted him to know that it was a naval officer he was shooting at, if he opened up again.

"Still," said King, "I'm going."

"Fine, but once we're down there, you're going to have to take orders from me."

"I've done that before," she said.

Tynan nodded and then looked back at the TV screen. Nothing new was going on. Police officers were running around, maybe trying for a chance to look brave on television. The reporter, looking scared, was talking to a police lieutenant now who was talking about having the suspect pinned down. They were going to take their time and make sure that no one died who didn't have to die.

Tynan shook his head. Shove a TV camera in the face of some people and they said the dumbest things. He'd seen it in Vietnam. An officer who was normally quiet, reserved, was thrown in front of a camera and suddenly he was John Wayne at the Alamo. It made everyone look stupid.

There was a knock at the door. Tynan shrugged and wondered how Harison had gotten there so quickly. When he opened it, he saw Jacobs. He pushed by Tynan and then stopped in front of the TV.

"Oh, you've got it on."

"Harison is on his way over and we're going down there," said Tynan.

"Then you already know that it's Davis."

Tynan stared at the man and said, "We don't know it, but we suspect it."

"Don't worry about it, it is."

"Shit," said Tynan. "How do you know?"

"Because he was talking about assassinating someone with a high-powered rifle and asked what I thought would be best for the job. Obviously, he missed his target, but he's not giving it up yet."

"Now why do you say that?"

"Because no one has been shot yet and Davis is still there, waiting for the target to show himself."

"Maybe we can talk him out of it," said King.

Tynan shook his head and thought about the conversation about Hitler. Davis was a man with a mission, and as a SEAL, he would not stop until he was either dead or the mission was accomplished.

Harison arrived then and pushed open the door. "You ready?" he asked.

Tynan grabbed his jacket and said, "As ready as I'm going to be."

Harison turned and headed down the hallway. Tynan closed the door as soon as everyone was out and then followed. As he approached the parking lot, he knew, just knew, that it wasn't going to be easy to get Davis down without someone dying.

14

For fifteen minutes, not a shot had been fired. Everything was held as it was, with the police maneuvering on the street, trying to get all the civilians out of the line of fire. They were working to evacuate the buildings so that no one would get hurt by stray bullets if the gunman decided to start shooting out windows.

Davis watched it, being careful not to expose himself to the police guns below him. He watched the parking lot, but none of the officers ran into it and no one came out. Bainbridge was still down there somewhere, hiding. All Davis had to do was wait for him to show himself.

As he watched, he noticed that it was strangely quiet around them. The heartbeat of the city seemed to have been stilled. There wasn't the undercurrent of sound that was always present. The rumbling trucks, the squeal of tires, the horns and shouts and music were all gone now. It was almost as if they were in a western where it was suddenly too quiet.

"It's not going to work," said Davis suddenly. "Not going to work at all."

"Then what are we going to do?" asked Sullivan.

"One of us has got to get out of here and complete the mission later. It's important that we stop Bainbridge. Maybe if you go to the police now and tell them what he did, it'll be enough to stop him in the future." But even as he said it, he knew that it wasn't going to be enough. Bainbridge could dodge a single account of assaulting a woman, especially as he began the climb to political power. People would ignore it. The second one, the second case, was the one where they would begin to listen, taking it all seriously, but even then he might be able to buy his way clear.

"How?" she asked. "They're going to arrest the both of us when they get up here."

"No," said Davis. "You tell them that I took you as a hostage. There was nothing you could do about it because I was heavily armed and was going to kill you."

"No," she said. "I couldn't do that. They'd throw you in jail."

"Rachel, they're already going to throw me in jail no matter what you say or do. One of us has to be free to act."

"But if I say you kidnapped me, held me hostage, they'll just hold you longer."

"Hell, it won't make any difference."

"No."

Davis shrugged. He got to his knees and peered over the wall. The street was filled with cops. They were running all over the place, pointing and directing and jockeying for position. On the rooftops opposite of him, he saw officers crouched behind air-conditioning units, vents and machinery over elevator shafts. There were ten, twelve men he could have hit, if he'd wanted to shoot police officers.

Again, he thought that he had to slow them down. Keep them from getting to him for a while, though he couldn't have explained what good that was going to do. He glanced at Sullivan and warned her.

"They're going to start pouring some lead up here. Better keep your head down."

As she fell flat, he aimed at two police officers on the rooftop opposite him, just over four-hundred yards away. There was a thin metal rod that looked like a radio antenna. Davis aimed at it and squeezed off a shot. The round hit the rod and severed it. As it fell to the rear, the two officers were up and moving. One to the left and one to the right. Both dived for cover, rolling behind either the air conditioner or a short brick wall. Davis could still see one of them but neither of them fired at him.

He moved to the right, looked down at the street and flattened another tire of the squad car there. As he fired, so did the police below, their handguns popping in the distance sounding like cap guns. He didn't bother to duck, knowing that he was far outside their effective range. He watched them all scrambling for cover again.

"That'll hold them for a while," said Davis. He sat down, his back to the wall and looked at Sullivan.

"If Bainbridge moves, you won't see him."

"Too late now," said Davis. "He's either gotten clear and we missed it, or he's not going to move until we've been taken. Either killed or captured."

Two rounds struck the top of the wall, spraying a fine gray dust. One round whined off into the distance. The other hit the building and dropped to the deck.

"I never expected it to be like this," she said.

"We have got to make a few plans," said Davis. "I don't want to think that I've thrown away my life for nothing. You've got to get clear and stop Bainbridge."

"How?"

"You were my prisoner. Nothing you could do about it," said Davis again.

"What if they check with the gun store. They'll know that I wasn't being held there."

"Then you tell them that I told you that if you didn't act

normal I'd kill you and anyone in the store. You had no choice in the matter. You had to cooperate in the store or a lot of innocent people would have died.''

"Okay," she said. "Okay." There wasn't much conviction in her voice.

"You're going to have to trust me on this one," said Davis. "The point is that we stop Bainbridge. That's all that's important."

"Okay," she repeated, her voice dull.

"First, I'm going to have to tie you up. When the police get here, it'll add to the authenticity of your story."

"I don't think so," she said.

Davis crawled around to where she was. The firing from the street and the rooftops had tapered until it was only sporadic. They could hear the popping of the hand guns and the bull horn instructions, but it was almost as if it had nothing to do with them. The rounds weren't coming close.

"Don't worry, it'll be all right."

She sat up then and looked into his eyes. "I don't understand any of this now. It's like . . . like . . ." She let her voice trail off.

Davis knew exactly what she was trying to say. The events had swept them up and carried them along. Neither of them was a murderous person. Davis hadn't been able to understand how a man could lie in wait in ambush to shoot a politician. Now he was doing exactly the same thing, though Bainbridge was not yet a politician.

"It's like a bad dream," Davis finished for her. "Except when you wake up, Bainbridge will still exist, still be a threat. We've got to make sure there is one of us left to get him, somehow, someway."

She reached over and hugged him. She held him tight, not wanting to let go, even as another bullet struck the building. Finally she sat back and said, "Okay, I'll do what you say. We'll get him."

Davis touched his lips with the back of his hand and then said, "Roll onto your stomach and put your hands behind your back."

She did as told and Davis stripped his web belt. He touched her and then asked, "Are you ready?"

"No, but go ahead."

They were stopped four blocks away by a police officer wearing an orange vest and standing in the middle of the street. There was a police car parked behind him, across the road. As they stopped, he came up to the window on the driver's side.

"You'll have to detour," he said. "We're having some trouble up ahead."

"Yes, officer," said Tynan. "Have you been able to identify the gunman yet?"

"No."

"We may know him. We'd like a chance to help if we could," said Tynan.

The police officer turned and waved another man forward. They talked for a moment and then the second officer leaned down. "You think you know the man?"

"It's possible."

"All right. You follow me, and when I stop, you pull in right behind me."

"Got it," said Tynan.

The police officer ran over to his car as the first man got out of the way. Tynan pulled around, waited and then fell in behind the police vehicle.

"What are you going to tell them if we're wrong?" asked Jacobs.

"I'll tell them that we're sorry. We made a mistake."

They drove along streets that were deserted. No people and no traffic. They made one turn and the police car pulled to the curb. As the officer got out, so did Tynan.

"What do we do?" asked Jacobs.

"Wait here until I get a handle on this thing. Once we get some more information, we can decide what we're going to do about it."

The police officer came over and said, "Have the rest of the people wait right here. You follow me."

Tynan nodded.

They moved out, staying close to the side of the building. They turned a corner and Tynan saw a police van sitting in the middle of the street, the rear doors open. Inside were three men, a rack of radio equipment and a couple of TV monitors. One of the men got out and came toward them.

"What you got, Sergeant?"

"Man here claims to know who the gunman is, Lieutenant."

The police commander looked at Tynan and said, "That right?"

"I have a suspicion. Anyone been hurt yet?"

"We've been lucky. So far he's missed, but he's come close a couple of times."

"If it's who I think it is, no one has been hit because he's decided not to hit anyone."

"Then what's the point of all this?" asked the police lieutenant.

"Good question."

"And another one is who are you?"

Tynan nodded and said, "Sorry. I'm Lieutenant Mark Tynan of the United States Navy and I think the man you have trapped up there is one of my men."

"You have any idea what he's doing up there?"

"I haven't the foggiest notion," Tynan lied. "But if it is one of my men, you won't get to him until he's ready for you to get to him."

"Now what in hell is that? Some kind of threat?"

"No, just the facts. He's trained in this sort of thing. I'll bet there isn't more than one or two ways to get up there and he'll have them both covered. If he's not on the highest ground around, he's got the highest that anyone can get to. One or two well-placed shots from him, and you'll have to scatter for cover."

"He up there to prove something?"

Tynan shrugged. "I don't know why he's up there, but you won't get him until he's ready. If it's my man, I might be able to talk him down."

The cop stood there staring at Tynan as if he hated him. He waited for Tynan to drop his eyes, and when that didn't happen, the police lieutenant said, "Well, let's get around there and see if we can get this guy's identity. If you're right, that gives us a leg up."

"Let's go and see what we can learn."

They moved to the corner. Around it, Tynan could see a police car sitting on two flat tires. The emergency light bar on the top had taken a hit that had shattered it. Three policemen crouched behind it, but they weren't paying much attention to anything around them.

Tynan looked up at the parapet around the tower. There was some visible bullet damage to it, but there didn't seem to be anyone on it.

"Gunman is up there."

Tynan nodded. "Just as I said. He's got the high ground and there's no way for you to get at him. Only thing is, I don't see an obvious route of escape. Can't believe he'd let himself get trapped up there."

"We still don't know if it's your man," said the police lieutenant.

"No, we don't."

Using his web belt, Davis bound Sullivan's arms behind her. He looped it around her elbows and drew it tight until her elbows touched. That done, he took off his shirt and then his T-shirt and tore it into thin strips, binding her wrists and then her ankles.

"I know that it's going to be uncomfortable, but it's got to look real."

"It's all right," she said, but it didn't sound like it was all right.

Davis rolled her over and helped her sit up. He picked her up and moved her to the side, away from the door that led into the building. He set her down, leaning her against the wall. He wanted to kiss her then, but didn't.

As he turned away, the vision of Bainbridge came again. He was standing with the generals and the Secret Service men in the War Room. There were people crying and warning lights flashing all over. There were shouts of panic and there were a couple of shots as people went berserk, wanting to end the war before it got started.

All that they had done during the day was not going to prevent Bainbridge from finding his destiny. Even the trick, with Sullivan portrayed as a hostage, was not enough. Davis didn't know if the police failed to believe it or if she was powerless to stop Bainbridge later. All he knew was that Bainbridge was going to end up launching the war.

Again, it seemed that the future couldn't be changed. He wondered if he should leave her there and try to shoot his way clear. He might be able to make it out, but then the image of Bainbridge came again and he was still in charge in the War Room, ordering his generals to launch the missiles. It seemed that he too was powerless.

He moved away from Sullivan and then glanced back at her. Her posture was stiff. She looked uncomfortable with her arms bound the way they were, but the police had to believe she was a hostage. Even if she couldn't stop Bainbridge, it would keep her out of jail, and that was something. Not much but something.

He picked up his rifle and glanced down into the street. He saw movement down there but no one seemed interested in shooting at him now. It was quiet down there.

He dropped to the deck and then peeked over the wall at the roof opposite them. There were more police up there, armed with M-16s and hunting rifles. They were speading out, getting ready to take him.

And then a voice boomed from the street. "This is Lieutenant Tynan. Is that you Davis?"

He stood up and looked down into the street. He saw the lieutenant crouched behind the police car and thought that there might be a way to salvage it. Rachel might be powerless to stop Bainbridge, and he might have screwed it up by not thinking it through, but the lieutenant could get to Bainbridge. Tynan was the answer. He just had to convince the lieutenant to do something about it.

He crouched again and looked at Rachel. "If anything happens to me, you get to Lieutenant Tynan; he's here now. You get to him and tell him everything you know. Give him the notebook and tell him about Bainbridge. Tell him everything about the man and maybe he can do something about it."

When she nodded her understanding, he stood up then to wave at Tynan, to tell him that he was going to surrender. It was now all over, as long as he had the chance to talk to the lieutenant there was no reason to keep it going.

There was a single shot from one of the rooftops and Davis was thrown to the rear. He hit the side of the building and bounced off. There was a burning pain in his upper chest and it was hard to breathe. A warm liquid was spreading across his chest and his vision began to fade as the fire spread through his upper chest and his heart hammered. He tried to sit up, but the pain was too great. He tried to roll over to push himself up but couldn't do it. He thought about the old saying that you never heard the one that got you, but that wasn't true. He'd heard it. Felt it first, but then he'd heard the shot.

In the distance, he heard a woman screaming and didn't know what had happened.

15

When the shot was fired, Tynan dropped to the ground. He turned, looking to the rear, at one of the rooftops there, searching for the gunman. He didn't see anyone up there who might have fired.

"What the fuck?" demanded Tynan.

The police lieutenant, who was crouched by the open door of the car, said, "I don't know."

Then they heard the woman screaming. A faint, distant voice. Tynan was on his feet. He ran around the car, leaped over a trash can and hit the wall. Three police stood there, all of them scanning the rooftops opposite them, looking for the officer who had fired.

"How do I get up there?"

One of the officers looked at him, his face blank, as if he didn't understand English.

Tynan grabbed the man's vest and jerked him around. "How do I get up there?"

"In here. Elevator to the roof. But you can't go up there now."

Tynan pushed past the man, opened the door and ran to the bank of elevators. He pushed the button, and then had to wait. He turned, spotted the stairway and was tempted. He could run up the stairs. He could get moving. But in the long run it would be slower. He spun and hit the button again, knowing that it wouldn't speed the elevator. It was coming as fast as the electrical motor could work.

"Come on," he hissed. "Come on."

Two police officers entered the lobby then, one of them dressed in black, wearing a bulletproof vest and a black baseball cap. "Hey, you."

The elevator arrived with a loud bong of a bell. Tynan stepped in and hit the button to take him to the top floor. As the doors closed, the police officers ran toward him. But then he was on his way up.

On the top floor, he stood for a moment and then saw the exit signs that lead to the stairway. He ran to it, entered and continued up. Far below him he heard the police officers running up the stairs, chasing him.

Tynan came to another door and found himself on the rooftop. He hesitated for a moment and turned. Across the street, he could see a dozen cops moving on the rooftops there. Each was armed with an M-16 or a rifle. They had left their cover and were advancing carefully, almost as if they were an infantry company moving on a treeline occupied by the enemy. They were ready for trouble.

Tynan turned and saw the rusting ladder that lead up to the parapet. He ran toward it, hesitated again and then began to climb. As he reached the top, he heard the woman crying and then spotted Davis. He was lying on the deck, on his back, his head against the wall of the building. There was blood on his shirt and under his body. A lot of blood.

As he scrambled over the top, the woman said, "Help him. Help him."

Tynan ignored her. He crouched near Davis and saw that he was still alive. His skin was waxy, unnatural-looking. His breathing was rapid and shallow. Tynan put a hand over his chest, pushing slightly, and Davis began to breathe easier.

The man's eyes flutterd open and he said, "Fucked it up, sir."

"What in hell were you trying to accomplish? You didn't even leave yourself an escape route."

Davis smiled weakly. "Didn't figure I'd need it. Figured to be out before the cops arrived."

"Christ, man."

"Is he going to be all right?" asked the woman.

Tynan glanced at her and saw that her arms were bound. "Who are you?"

"Never mind me. Get him some help."

"Room key, sir. Get my room key." He coughed then and fell silent.

"Never mind that," said Tynan.

Davis reached up with his left hand and grabbed Tynan's shoulder. He tried to pull him closer. "It's up to you now, sir. You've got to stop him."

"Who?"

"Hitler," said Davis.

Tynan was going to say that he wasn't making sense, but he understood. Davis believed that he had found someone who was going to turn out worse than Hitler.

"You take it easy now . . ."

"Rachel can help. She knows, but you've got to take care of it."

One of the police officers poked his head over the top of the wall then. He looked at the scene, climbed to the parapet and picked up the sniper's rifle.

"Get an ambulance," said Tynan.

"Just a minute here . . ."

Tynan glanced up at the man and roared. "You get an ambulance now!"

"Yes, sir." He turned and yelled down. "We need an ambulance."

Tynan looked down at Davis. There was sweat on his

face. His eyes were closed. Tynan could see the pulse throbbing in his neck but didn't think the man would last long.

For a moment, Davis was conscious, seeming to be lucid. "You can't change it," he said. "I tried. You've got to."

"Who's the woman?" asked the cop as he climbed onto the parapet.

Tynan looked at her and then up at the police officer. "I have no idea. Why don't you untie her. I think this man was holding her hostage."

"Crazy fucker," said the policeman as he moved toward Sullivan.

There was a pounding on the door and the police moved to it, pulling the wedge free. More policemen, weapons drawn, spilled onto the parapet, but there was nothing for them to do now. They spread out, looking for evidence, trying not to kick the shell cases around.

"Looks like he was preparing for a siege," said one of the officers.

The lieutenant who had brought Tynan into the area asked, "You know the man?"

"Yes."

"We'll need to get a statement from you." He looked at the woman. "Who are you?"

"Rachel Sullivan. He was . . . he had taken . . . I was his hostage."

"Fine."

"The ambulance?" asked Tynan. He still held his hand over the chest wound, pressing harder to stop the bleeding.

"On its way."

The police lieutenant pointed to two of his men and said, "Why don't you take her down to the street and put her into one of the cars." He pointed at her and said, "We'll need a statement."

"Maybe she should go to the hospital," said Tynan. "Just to make sure she's okay."

In the distance came the wail of the ambulance siren.

The police lieutenant looked at the scene and said, "Christ, what a mess."

In the ambulance, on the way to the hospital, Davis came around again. He glanced up, at the bags of drugs hanging above him, at the medic in white, and then at Tynan, seated close to him. He looked at the lieutenant and said, "You'll have to take care of it now."

Tynan moved, crouching next to the stretcher. "What in hell are you talking about?"

Davis reached over and tried to touch Tynan. The lieutenant took the wounded man's hand and asked again, "What are you talking about?"

The medic was there, watching. Davis looked away, out the window, and knew that it wasn't worth the effort. He could see the future, but he couldn't change it. There was no way to convince Tynan that Bainbridge had to be stopped. And even if he could, there was no way that Tynan could take care of it. He'd learned that with his attempt.

He turned back, coughed and said, "Get to my room first. Get my notebook."

"I'll do what I can," said Tynan.

"And you'll try to stop Bainbridge?"

Tynan stared at him for a moment and then said, "I'll do what I can."

Davis closed his eyes and the scene in the War Room swam in front of him again. Bainbridge surrounded by the men, the generals, the computers. There was someone crying openly, noisily, as Bainbridge ordered the first, preemptive strike. It was the same vision that he'd had over and over. Bainbridge, the man who didn't deserve to be President, standing there as the President, ordering the destruction of the Earth with the casualness that most men used ordering lunch.

Davis appealed again, locking his eyes on Tynan. "Promise that you'll try to stop him."

"I promise," said Tynan.

But the scene didn't change. Bainbridge was still in control and the Earth was about to be plunged into the nuclear holocaust. Davis tried to see beyond it, to what the Earth would be like. Would the planet be nothing more than a radioactive ash, inhabited by grotesque creatures caused by the radiation? Or would it be a barren rock, stripped of its atmosphere and its life by the war? He couldn't tell.

He felt weak. Even with the promise that Tynan would try, nothing changed. Bainbridge would somehow survive to become President and that would mean the end of the United States, of civilization.

He couldn't change the future. It was there, already written and as immutable as the past. That was why people could glimpse it with psychic abilities. There was no free will and free determination. It was already scripted, and the people moved through the settings according to that script. Forewarned was not forearmed. It merely meant that there were frustrated people who were powerless to change the foreordained.

Davis rolled over and hoped that death would come soon because he wouldn't be able to stand it in prison, knowing that the Earth was about to die. Death was preferrable to a life, a short life in prison.

When they arrived at the hospital, Davis was wheeled into an operating room almost immediately. Police officers swarmed all over, fighting through the crowds of reporters, trying to learn what had happened. Tynan was confronted by three policemen who demanded to know what had happened and what Davis had said to him.

Tynan shrugged and said, "Not all that much. I think he was delirious the whole time."

He and Rachel were questioned separately, together, and then handed over to the reporters who demanded more from them. Tynan said little and Sullivan repeated the story that Davis had given her. She was a hostage.

"Why was he up there shooting?"

"I don't know."

"What motivated him?"

"I don't know."

"Was it random or did he have a target?"

"I don't know."

It continued on in that vein until Tynan decided that enough was enough. He pulled Sullivan to the side and they escaped into a small room that was used by doctors to give the bad news to the families of patients. As they sat down, there was a knock on the door and Jacobs stuck his head in.

"Got a car here when you're ready to get out."

"Fine," said Tynan. "Find the police officer in charge and learn what his plans are."

"Yes, sir."

As the door closed, Tynan turned to Sullivan and said, "Now what can you tell me? I know that Davis didn't take you hostage. You were working with him and he gave you an out so that you could finish the job."

Tears filled her eyes and spilled. She glanced at the floor and then the ceiling and finally said, "It was Bainbridge. He, Dennis, told me that Bainbridge was an evil man."

"So, out of the blue, you joined in this . . . murder attempt," said Tynan.

"It wasn't like that," she protested. She told him the

whole story then, from the moment she'd met Davis at the pizza parlor to the moment Tynan had appeared on the ladder.

Tynan sat back, leaning against the rear of the couch, looking up at the ceiling, feeling completely drained. "That's one hell of a story," he said.

"Then you'll get Bainbridge?"

Tynan thought about everything that had passed in the last few days. The discussions of ESP and precognition and the history of the human race. He thought about killing Hitler before he could condemn the Earth to a destructive war and thought about changing the future. Did anyone have the right to do it? Of course, to do it, you had to know what the future held, and that was the real problem.

"Bainbridge does exist," said Tynan, amazed at that one bit of information. It wasn't something that Davis had imagined. He'd seen an evil man and according to Sullivan, the Bainbridge they'd tried to shoot was an evil man.

Sullivan looked at Tynan then. She studied his face and his eyes and finally asked, "What are you going to do?"

"That's the question, isn't it?" said Tynan. "I don't have the faintest notion."

"But you're going to get Bainbridge?"

"I don't know." He thought that there was more that he should say, but didn't know what it was. It was the only answer that he had.

"I don't know," he repeated.

16

Tynan unlocked the door of the motel room and stood back. He didn't want to enter it, but there was no reason not to. Davis had told him to get the notebook before the police learned about it and impounded it. The notebook would explain everything, the man had said.

He entered the room and looked around quickly. Clothes were hung in the closet. There was a suitcase sitting on the dresser, open. There was a pair of shoes by the bed and a jacket hung over the back of a chair. There was no notebook lying out in the open.

Tynan entered the room and closed the door. He stood there for a moment, feeling like an intruder. He took a step forward and stopped. He glanced into the bathroom, where Davis had left his shaving kit.

Rather than begin the search, Tynan sat on the bed. He stared at the floor and then at the suitcase. Without having to look, he knew that the notebook was in there. It was the only place that made any sense.

He stood and moved to the case. There was a pouch on the top of the case and in it was the notebook. A cheap, spiral notebook like kids carried to school. Not the thing that you'd expect to find holding the future of the human race. Tynan pulled it out and opened it.

Apparently Davis had anticipated problems in dealing with Bainbridge. The first page warned that he might fail and that the duty would then fall to whoever held the notebook and the knowledge. Davis had written that this was like finding a notebook that chronicled the rise and fall of Adolph Hitler before the beginning of the Second World War. Here was a chance to spare the world, spare the human race the misery that one man could inflict.

"But there's no proof," said Tynan. He then closed the notebook and moved toward the door. He had the one thing that Davis was afraid would fall into the wrong hands. Before he closed the door on his way out, he made sure that it would lock. Then, in the hallway, he turned to the left, hurrying toward the parking lot.

As he reached the car, King opened the door and said, "You get it?"

"Right here." Tynan climbed into the passenger side.

King started the engine and moved toward the street. "What's it say?"

"I haven't read that much of it," said Tynan, "but it looks to be a diary of some kind." He flipped through it, saw the dates on it and added, "A future diary."

"What?"

Tynan shrugged. He read a couple of the passages and said, "He seems to have listed every vision or prediction that he's made or had or whatever. Everything up to and including this Bainbridge launching the next world war."

King pulled into traffic and then stopped at a light. She glanced at the book and said, "What do you think?"

"I don't know. This thing is frightening if what it says is true. What I'm reminded of is those notebooks that what's-his-name kept. The journals he kept while stalking his victims. He wrote down all the information he found about the target before he went out to get him."

"But that's not like this."

"No," agreed Tynan, "but I'm holding the motivation for the crime."

They started again and she asked, "What's the crime? Discharging a firearm in the city limits?"

Tynan stared at her and shrugged. "I don't know. They'll probably have a whole shopping list of them. Reckless endangerment springs to mind. Attempted murder, though with this in my hands, it's going to be hard to prove that."

"What'll happen to him? To Davis." She pulled into the parking lot of the motel.

"Again, I don't know. Those cops were pretty sore about the whole thing and I don't blame them. He'll probably end up with a ten-year sentence and be out in three. Something like that. The whole point is that no one was hurt."

"What about the Navy?"

"Oh," said Tynan, "he's out. Bad-conduct discharge, especially if there is jail time. He might have to put in some time in a Navy brig, but I kind of doubt that."

King said, "Let me see that notebook."

Tynan handed it over. "It's quite a document."

She read some of it and then flipped to the end, reading the three pages devoted to Bainbridge and the end of three-quarters of the human race on Earth. When she finished she said, "Jesus. He believed this, didn't he?"

"I would think that his actions today proved that."

"What are you going to?" She turned to face him. The engine was still idling and the radio was playing softly in the background.

Tynan turned and stared out the windshield. He thought again about Hitler and how it would have been possible, just possible, to have spared the world the Second World War. That was if someone knew what Hitler was going to do. Now Tynan found himself in that position. Maybe.

"The problem, as I see it," said Tynan, "is that we

don't, I don't know if he's right. Maybe all this''—he pointed at the notebook—''is some kind of delusion. Bainbridge might be an innocent man.''

"Do you believe that?" asked King.

"Shit, I don't know. There are so many things about this whole affair that I can't explain. Sumner-Gleason told me that Davis scored a hundred out of a hundred on the standard PSI test. No one ever does that.''

"So he has some talent.''

"Agreed," said Tynan. "But what kind of talent? We're not talking about being good at guessing games here. We're talking about commiting a murder based solely on another man's delusion.''

"He tried to do something about it," said King.

"Yes, but it was his delusion, it's not mine. Right now I just don't know what to do.''

She turned back and looked into the notebook. "Good Lord. Do you know what all this stuff means?"

"Some of it makes sense, like the fall of Saigon in 1975. Looks like the communists will rename it Ho Chi Minh City. And the invasion of Grenada in what, 1982 or '83. That makes some sense. I don't understand the Challenger disaster, though it appears a spacecraft explodes. Or this AIDS thing. Some kind of worldwide disease that sweeps across the planet in the late 1980s.''

King grinned and said, "Well the Cubs fans will have something to cheer about in 1984. They get into the play-offs, only to lose to San Diego.''

"The book is rich in predictions," said Tynan. "Hundreds of them.''

"Seems to me that this whole thing is the answer to the question," she said. She closed it and set it on the seat between them.

"I know what you're thinking," said Tynan. "We hang on to the notebook and see if the predictions come true.

If some of them do we then decide what to do about Bainbridge.''

"There are so many of them, that we could easily determine if he was right or wrong."

"What if we're not sure," said Tynan. "What if only some of them come true?"

"What do you mean by that?"

"What if some of the things come close. Maybe Saigon doesn't fall in 1975, as he claims but in 1976. Maybe in January. Close, but not quite right."

"Then that would mean that he could be wrong about Bainbridge," said King. "Maybe Bainbridge is the salvation of the nation, not the destroyer."

"It's the shadings that I'm concerned about. We're relying on Davis to have interpreted everything perfectly, but he might have seen something wrong. Or maybe seen it right but not understood it."

King shook her head. "Then there is no answer. But we have here a document that could prove to be one of the most valuable ever written. We can't just toss it aside and forget all about it."

"No," said Tynan. "We've got to hang on to it and study it. Look for flaws in it. About the only thing we have going for us on this one is time. We can sit back and see if he's right. If he hits on the majority of it, then we're going to have to do something about Bainbridge."

"Providing that we can do anything to change the future," said King.

Tynan picked up the notebook and rifled the pages again. "If we know about it, then we can change it," he said.

"Isn't that what Davis tried," said King. "He knew what had to be done and he failed to get it done."

Tynan nodded his agreement and then added, "But he went about it all wrong. Tried to take care of it today when it didn't have to be done today. Besides, he failed to stop Bainbridge today, but that doesn't mean he failed totally. He did get us interested in the project.''

"Which means we're going to do something about Bainbridge?"

"It means," said Tynan, "that we're going to study the situation, and if it warrants action on our part, then we're going to take it. It means that if his other predictions come true, then we're going to do something about Bainbridge."

"Providing we can," cautioned King.

"Providing we can."

Davis came awake suddenly. There were huge bandages on his chest and around his arm. There were bottles suspended in the air over him and the quiet beep of a machine that monitored his heart rate.

Again he tried to see into the future but this time he failed. Nothing was there. He felt his heart skip and his stomach grow cold. There was no way to save the human race because he couldn't change the future.

And then suddenly he realized that he was wrong. The future wasn't written in stone, immutable; it was something pliable as clay. It could be molded into a dozen, a hundred, a thousand directions, if a man had the knowledge to do it. He'd failed to stop Bainbridge, not because the future was a rigid structure but because he had rushed into action. There was no reason to attack today. Tomorrow, next week, would have been soon enough, as long as he knew what was going to happen.

But he knew the future could be changed because he had already done it. He had seen his death in Vietnam in a year and now knew that was not going to be the case. He was dying now, he knew it as surely as he knew everything else. He wouldn't live to see the Vietnam jungle. And if he survived now, he would spend the next few years in jail. There was no way for him to end up on that patrol to die. None whatsoever.

And then he reached out again, trying to find Bainbridge in the future. Trying to find the scene in the War Room, but it was no longer there. It was gone, as if it had been erased from the history of the world.

Tynan, he thought. The lieutenant had finally made a decision about it. He'd read the notebook and there was enough there that the lieutenant would act on the information. Tynan would do something that prevented Bainbridge from gaining power. Maybe he'd use some of his friends in the government to blackball Bainbridge, or maybe he'd just assassinate him. Davis couldn't see that. He just knew that Bainbridge would never have the power to order a preemptive strike. He would never become President of the United States. Something had changed.

Davis opened his eyes and saw two figures standing near him. Blonde-headed figures who he thought he recognized. An older sister who had died when she was eighteen and a woman that Davis had loved once, a woman who had moved away before they had a chance to be together.

A peaceful feeling washed over him, because he knew his task was finished, his mission over. He had entrusted it to another who would see it through to its conclusion. There was no longer a reason to fight for life, no longer a reason to hang on.

He closed his eyes and was aware of the women touching him. The pain was gone then. It evaporated and he was tranquil. He felt himself sit up and then swing his feet from the bed. The tubes that had run into his body, into his arm and into his nose, did not bother him. He stood up and grinned at his sister, holding out his arms to hug her.

He wasn't aware that the heart machine had stopped beeping and was emitting a nerve-shattering squeal. He didn't know that two doctors and three nurses burst into the room and tried to resuscitate him. As he moved off with his sister and old girlfriend, he didn't know that one of the doctors had pulled a sheet over his face or that a nurse had shut off the monitoring equipment.

None of that made any difference to him because his job was done. Now it was time for the reward.